His anger is too strong and too familiar to let go of.

If Joseph were a shaman like those in his grandfather's stories, he would change all the white-skinned men to white-headed eagles that would soar high above the village, and then he would slice their wings from their bodies so they would plummet to the ground. And the people of the village would tiptoe around them, pointing in horror, fearful of partaking of the tainted meat, leaving their twisted forms for the scavenging foxes.

But there was no longer any shaman's magic, only the schooling of the white man. Dull routines, endless rules, outside obligations piled one upon the other—burdens of progress that weighed upon Joseph's mind as he stood looking out across the frozen river, breathing heavy in the frosty air.

Joseph's troubles swirled within him like a backwater eddy—the money, his former job, his spoiled relationship with Elena, the intrusive school teacher. Anger at all of them frothed to the surface, and he broke into a dead run to escape it before it covered him completely.

D1622397

OTHER PUFFIN BOOKS YOU MAY ENJOY

A Distant Enemy

Deb Vanasse

March 21, 2000

PUFFIN BOOKS

"Do Not Go Gentle Into That Good Night" (excerpt of three stanzas) by Dylan Thomas, from *The Poems of Dylan Thomas*. Copyright © 1952 by Dylan Thomas. Reprinted by permission of New Directions Publishing Corp.

PUFFIN BOOKS
Published by the Penguin Group
Penguin Putnam Books for Young Readers,
345 Hudson Street, New York, New York 10014, U.S.A.
Penguin Books Ltd, 27 Wrights Lane, London W8 5TZ, England
Penguin Books Australia Ltd, Ringwood, Victoria, Australia
Penguin Books Canada Ltd, 10 Alcorn Avenue, Toronto, Ontario, Canada M4V 3B2
Penguin Books (N.Z.) Ltd, 182-190 Wairau Road, Auckland 10, New Zealand

Penguin Books Ltd, Registered Offices: Harmondsworth, Middlesex, England

First published in the United States of America by Lodestar Books,
an affiliate of Dutton Children's Books, a division of Penguin Books USA Inc., 1997
Published by Puffin Books,
a member of Penguin Putnam Books for Young Readers, 1999

1 3 5 7 9 10 8 6 4 2

THE LIBRARY OF CONGRESS HAS CATALOGED THE LODESTAR EDITION AS FOLLOWS:
Vanasse, Deb.
A distant enemy/by Deb Vanasse—1st ed.
p. cm.
Summary: Fourteen-year-old Joseph, part Yup'ik Eskimo and part white,
struggles to maintain his people's ancient culture as the western
world encroaches on his Alaska village.
ISBN 0-525-67549-3 (alk. paper)
1. Yupik Eskimos—Ethnic identity—Juvenile fiction. [Yupik Eskimos—Ethnic
identity—Fiction. 2. Eskimos—Ethnic identity—Fiction. 3. Alaska—Fiction.]
I. Title.
PZ7.V2755Di 1997 [Fic]—dc20 96-23428 CIP AC

Puffin Books ISBN 0-14-038670-X

Printed in the United States of America

to Lynx and Jessica,
with love

ACKNOWLEDGMENTS

I would like to thank the members of SCBWI in Fairbanks, especially authors Claire Rudolf Murphy and Randy Stowell, who read the manuscript in its entirety. I am also grateful to my husband, Tim Vanasse, for his technical advice on the details of fishing, hunting, and trapping; and to Sophie Shield for her help with the Yup'ik words.

Most of all, my thanks to the people of the Yukon-Kuskokwim Delta who shared the richness of their lives with me and my family.

ONE

JOSEPH AND HIS GRANDFATHER sat without speaking in
the sixteen-foot wooden skiff on Long River, watching
a string of white plastic corks as they bobbed in the
ripples of brown water. Beneath the corks stretched
fifteen feet of net, its five-inch diamonds of mesh
reaching all the way to the heavy lead line, which
bumped along the mucky river bottom.

Joseph held a hand to his ear, to shield it from the
wind that pummeled cool air against it. The tundra
stretched in all directions beyond the river, a canvas of
browns and greens that faded into the gray August skies
along the horizon.

This flat, wet tundra of southwestern Alaska had been
home to Joseph's people, the Yup'ik Eskimos, for centuries. And for centuries, the rivers that snaked through
the land had yielded their fish. Joseph watched the
corkline intently. Far below the surface of the silty
water, a fish tangled in the net would cause movement
along the corkline as it struggled to free itself. At last,
one cork began to bob.

"*Neqerpak,*" Joseph said softly. A big silver salmon.
He looked over at his grandfather seated on the middle
bench of the boat and, not for the first time, felt large

by comparison. He already towered over the old man. Just this summer, when Joseph had turned fourteen, his grandfather had put him at the helm while they fished.

"Iii," his grandfather acknowledged, nodding his head in agreement. "Or maybe the fish is caught close to the surface." Just then a second cork along the forty-foot length of floating line began to bob, too, though with less force than the first.

"Our drying racks will be full yet." Joseph tried to reassure himself as well as his grandfather. By late summer, the racks that dotted the tundra along the river's edge should have been packed with gleaming fish, expertly cut and hung by the tails. But theirs, like most others in the village, was less than half full. Every year, it seemed, there were fewer and fewer fish in the river.

"Yet another." The old man pointed a crooked finger at a third bobbing cork. Joseph smiled. Perhaps a large school had swum into their net.

Five minutes passed, then ten. A gull careened overhead, a lone seabird gliding far inland in the moist air. The wind blew steady and soft across the tundra grasses. The three corks bobbed more slowly, less steadily now. No others joined them.

"Grandfather, we should pull in." Joseph tapped his fingers on one knee.

"Patience, boy. Wait a few moments more." His Yup'ik words sounded soft, like the wind rustling through the tundra grasses.

Joseph complied, but the movement of his fingers

betrayed his anxiety. The boat was drifting in toward shore now. A sandpiper scurried along the bank, pecking its long, thin beak at the river mud and calling out a loud, piercing cry.

"Where are the other fishermen today?" his grandfather asked idly. Joseph stiffened.

"Lazy, Ap'a," he replied. Joseph glanced at his grandfather for a reaction. The old man sat motionless, his dark eyes silent, his face unreadable.

Joseph knew why they were the solitary boat today. The CB radio, still preferred over the newer telephone lines for conveying news of interest to the whole village, had announced an emergency closure: no subsistence fishing, declared by the Fish and Game officials. There was to be no more harvest this season. *Akleng*, Joseph thought to himself. Too bad. This water, this fish, this land—did it belong to the Fish and Game troopers?

Already they had limited the king salmon harvest to just a few scattered days in June, and the chum salmon harvest to only a week and a half in July. When Joseph had heard the dismal broadcast of the closure for silver salmon just yesterday, his first impulse had been to go immediately to his grandfather, to cancel their fishing plans and bemoan the injustice.

But his irritation had grown quickly into defiance, and he had decided to keep news of the closure to himself. His grandfather, who often savored the quiet by keeping his CB off, had evidently heard nothing about the closure. The pair had gone fishing as planned.

The drone of an engine in the distance, too far away to be a boat motor, broke through the tundra silence.

3

Joseph scanned the skies. It was a plane, no more than a black speck in the sky, headed in their direction. The regular mail plane had already come and gone. Maybe it was a charter, but most villagers couldn't afford that, not with commercial fishing as bad as it was this year. Or maybe— Joseph pushed the thought aside.

"Grandfather, I think we should go in." Joseph began pulling in the net as he spoke, and the wet corkline piled beside his sneakered feet. He tugged hard against the pull of the first fish, still engaged in its unseen battle with the mesh.

His grandfather rose to join him as the fish came into view. In its struggle with impending death, the fish thrust its body from side to side, though its bright red hue and a hooked jaw marked the fish as a spawned-out salmon, its life already spent, ready to die. The flesh would be soft to eat, but at least it had deposited its eggs for the future.

Joseph clubbed the salmon on the head. The final shivers of life left its body as he and his grandfather expertly worked the net, untangling the fish where its thrashing fins and tail had wound tight in the filament. The wind whipped Grandfather's plaid shirt against his thin frame, but his dark, gnarled hands worked strong and sturdy beside Joseph's younger though sometimes fumbling fingers.

The engine sound grew louder, and Joseph looked up as he pulled the net in with more urgency. The plane was clearly in view now, a Cessna 180. He and his grandfather pulled in unison, and the second fish came over the side. This one was still shiny silver, and they clubbed and extracted it with little difficulty. But the third fish came up tangled near the lead line. It, too, was still bright silver, and it had fought hard for life, wrapping itself in and out of the diamond-shaped webs in defiance of its captors.

Joseph cursed the fish under his breath as he and his grandfather struggled to release it. The filament wound tight around its tail section. Together they pulled and stretched at the net and the slimy fish. At last the tail came loose, and they turned their attention to the head. Fish blood drizzled their hands as they worked the net at the gills, loosening each section with care. The plane was buzzing now, like a mosquito circling in the night, and Joseph's alarm grew into panic. What if it were a Fish and Game plane?

Before his grandfather had time to protest, Joseph pulled a jackknife from his shirt pocket and cut the remaining lines of net still wrapped tightly around the fish's hooked jaw. Mending the net would demand tedious effort, but Joseph didn't care. He jerked the last of the mesh into the boat, then pushed the idling motor into full throttle.

The sudden forward thrust forced the old man to his seat. His brow furrowed beneath his gray hair, and his dark, narrow eyes focused on his grandson. Joseph made himself stand tall and cold like a carved image, staring beyond his grandfather as he guided the boat down the river toward the village. Above them, the plane circled low, and the combined roar of both motors set his nerves on edge.

Joseph looked up for only a moment, not long enough

to confirm or deny his worst fear. He pinned his hopes on driving fast enough to obscure the license number on their tiny boat, just in case. He stared straight ahead again. The wooden floor of the skiff flexed as they pounded along the surface of the water, leaving the smell of gasoline and late summer salmon in its wake.

Two

When they reached the village, Joseph forced a sharp turn and ran the boat onto shore alongside a dozen other skiffs perched on the mucky beach. Napamiut stretched before them, a collection of scattered plywood houses in weathered hues of red, green, and blue hunkered low against an endless backdrop of land and sky and nestled into a curve of Long River.

The wind brought in a moist drizzle that cooled their hands and faces as they unloaded. Joseph threw the three big fish from the bottom of the boat into a white plastic five-gallon bucket and hoisted it out onto shore. He allowed himself only one quick glance in the direction of the runway. He couldn't see for sure, but he guessed that the plane had landed.

"Come on, Ap'a," Joseph said, forcing a smile. "We'll cut these and Mother can use one for fish stew tonight." He pushed a lock of curly black hair up under the rim of his red baseball cap.

Joseph's grandfather shook his head. He looked tired and small, staring at Joseph. Joseph suspected that the sudden rush from the river had left him bewildered, but the old man asked no questions. Instead, he turned and climbed the short path to the boardwalk, ambling slowly toward his one-room house that hung like a straggling bird off the east end of the village.

Joseph opened his mouth to call after him, but decided against it. Was he suspicious? Disappointed? Hurt? His grandfather, hardened into silence, was difficult to read. Maybe he was just tired. Anyway, nothing was wrong. They had just come in sooner and faster than normal.

The officials, if that's who they were, had no way of knowing them, Joseph told himself as he picked up the bucket of fish and headed for home. It was a good thing, too, because they could confiscate your boat and motor if they caught you fishing during a closed period. Anger swelled inside him like a wave. What right did they have?

Reaching the weathered entryway, Joseph flung open the door. The darkness of the musty storage area assaulted his senses, and he paused a moment to gather his thoughts.

He had originally intended to cut the fish at Grandfather's house, hanging them outside where no one was likely to notice. But now, here he was with three fish caught in a closed period, and a mother inside who listened to the CB and who likely was aware that there was to be no more fishing this season.

Never mind. He had learned lately that, if he used a loud voice and a rough manner, his mother offered little resistance. Joseph thrust himself through the inside door and slammed it behind him.

"Hush," Dora hissed, leaning forward from where she sat on the bed that served as a sofa. "It's the good part."

"Hush yourself," Joseph replied, glaring. "You guys watch too much TV anyway."

Dora rolled her eyes.

"Look!" Elsie exclaimed, pointing a finger. "There's the killer." A woman's shrill scream rang out from the TV perched on a wooden crate in the corner. Elsie pulled Sam, the youngest, close to her. His eyes were wide with terror.

Joseph shook his head. Ever since the village had put up a satellite dish, his brother and sisters had been glued to the set. They should be outside, running and playing and breathing in the freshness of the last days of summer.

The inside air was warm and damp from laundry strung to dry across another corner of the room. The house smelled of detergent and disinfectant, fish and seal oil—familiar smells to Joseph.

His mother was not in sight. Joseph set the bucket at his feet, but then thought twice and removed it to a dark corner of the entryway, where it would be half camouflaged among various raincoats, tools, and other buckets. Then he checked the bedroom, not a room, really, but a space separated from the rest by a partition.

Joseph's mother, despite the front-room noise, lay napping on a twin mattress on the floor. Her five-foot frame formed a graceful curve on the makeshift bed. Her long, dark hair fanned out behind her head, and her breath was light and even. In sleep, she looked helpless and childlike, not a force that Joseph need reckon with.

Not to waste the defiance he had invoked just in case his mother challenged him, Joseph turned and kicked the small truck his brother had left lying among other clutter on the weathered floor. It flew across the room, landing upside down where it hit the wall, its tires spinning. The kids huddled closer on the bed, but Joseph couldn't tell if they were reacting to his mood or to the blood-letting on the TV screen.

Feeling a bit calmer now, Joseph turned to dip water from the plastic barrel next to the refrigerator when a message came over the CB radio.

"Attention!" It was the soft, firm voice of Alexie John, the city manager. "Fish and Game officials are here to meet with residents concerning the recent emergency closure and other related issues. Gather at the community center in fifteen minutes." Alexie then repeated his message in Yup'ik, the guttural tones crackling over the CB channel.

Joseph's heart sank. And now Grandfather might know, too, if he had turned on his CB.

Joseph pulled out a chair and sat at the table, where an array of foods stayed spread all day: Sunny Jim jam, pilot bread, butter-flavored Crisco, strips of dry fish. He tore into one of the strips, chewing the tough flesh and savoring the thick oil on his tongue.

"Joseph, will you take me fishing?" Sam stretched himself off the bed and padded toward his brother, leaving the pounding TV background music as it built to a crescendo.

"Stupid!" Joseph glared at Sam. The boy stopped short, his smile wilting. "Didn't you just hear them say there's an emergency closure? Kass'aq rules!" he added, invoking the timeworn term for white people, which

10

could be used either as innocuous slang or a searing insult. He tore off another chunk of dry fish.

Sam ran back to the bed and hid his face in his hands. "He's only six. What does he know about emergency closures?" Dora chided.

Elsie pulled Sam up beside her, and they turned their attention back to the stalking madman on the TV screen.

Fifteen minutes until the meeting. Were the brown-shirted troopers on the way to Joseph's house right now, to take him in as an example before the whole village? Could they have picked out his boat as the offender from among the others on shore? Joseph didn't think so. There were three others almost exactly like it: home-made, wooden, painted dark marine green.

But if they narrowed it down to just those, and were checking on each of the owners . . . He remembered how hard he had worked last summer, helping his uncle during commercial fishing to earn enough to buy the 35-horse Johnson motor that now could end up in the hands of his latest enemy, the Alaska Department of Fish and Game.

They couldn't prove anything, though, unless of course they found the fresh fish in the bucket. Joseph pushed thoughts quickly through his head. He could cover the bucket with coats and mud boots and hope they didn't look too closely. Too bad his family didn't own a big chest freezer—he could throw them in whole.

Maybe he should move the bucket over to Elena Nicholai's porch across the way. He toyed with the thought. Joseph hated Elena's snippy voice and constant

11

prying. As children they had been friends, but now, at fourteen, she had turned into a constant nuisance. She was like her mother, a sharp-nosed woman who loved to spread gossip. There would be some satisfaction in getting her family in trouble. Was their boat green like his? He was trying to recall, when he heard footsteps and the opening of the outer door. Great, just great, Joseph thought.

Joseph rose to confront the brown-shirted intruders. But when the inside door swung open, he saw only his friend Simon Andrew. Short and wiry to Joseph's tall and muscular stance, Simon could hardly be mistaken for a brownshirt. Besides, Joseph realized as the pounding in his chest subsided, kass'aqs always knocked.

"Going to the meeting?" Simon asked with a grin. Simon was always grinning, it seemed, unless it was a rare occasion where deep respect was called for. His dark eyes sparkled behind wire-rimmed glasses. Simon's cheerfulness could be downright irritating.

"Oh, I don't know." Joseph tried to sound casual.

"Come on, let's go," Simon insisted. "I heard Alexie John is going to tell off those troopers."

That was lure enough for Joseph. The two boys headed out of the house and down the maze of boardwalks toward the community center. There would be a crowd, Joseph assured himself as they walked. He wouldn't stand out.

The river rolled alongside them as they skirted the village. Each plywood house stood on stubby pilings, lifted above the permafrost of the tundra. Most houses had a tiny steam bath, a snow machine or two, and a tilted clothesline nearby. Here, near the river, tall tundra grass filled in the yards, bent as always in the steady wind. The houses farther from the river had only low tundra foliage—mosses, lichens, and low berry bushes—surrounding them.

"Summer's over," Simon offered as they made their way past the old grade school buildings that loomed huge in pastel yellow beside the river. "School starts tomorrow."

Joseph breathed in deep, filling his lungs with the cool air that marked the changing of the seasons. Summer, always too short, was drawing quickly to a close. With this realization of time spent and lost, Joseph felt his temper rise to the surface.

"Same old stuff," he growled. "I hate school."

"But high school . . . will be different," Simon replied.

"Right. How different can it be? Same old people we've known since kindergarten, studying the same old kass'aq stuff."

"I haven't known them all since kindergarten," Simon reminded him, pushing up his glasses as they slid down his nose. After his father became a preacher, his family had left their home village and settled as outsiders in Napamiut. The memory of Simon as a new, awkward kid in the fourth grade came to Joseph. Villagers were slow to take in outsiders, even Eskimos from other villages, who more than likely were related to someone, if distantly, as Simon's family was to the Sams in Napamiut.

"In high school, we'll get to switch classes and teachers every hour," Simon offered, ever enthusiastic.

"Big deal. Three different teachers is all there'll be.

And we've known Mr. and Mrs. Kingston for years, even if they haven't been our teachers."

"Mr. Kingston is fun, though. He reminds me of a rabbit. We could play some good jokes on him," Simon suggested. Simon had a reputation for practical jokes, and Joseph often got in on the action. Once they had left a slimy blackfish wriggling in Elsie Charles's lunch bag and laughed for days over her horrified scream. Another time they had set up an elaborate avalanche of books from a shelf, triggered when their gray-haired eighth-grade teacher, plump Mrs. MacDonald, opened a desk drawer to search for her carefully hidden glasses. She had retired at the end of that year.

The boys passed by the grade school and the large fuel tanks at the river's edge, where the barge edged up once a year to fill drum after drum with oil for the winter. They took a sharp turn with the boardwalk to the right, away from the river, and dodged a preschooler with a crew cut as he careened by on his tiny two-wheeled bike.

"Maybe we should save our jokes for the new teacher. Have you seen him yet?" Joseph asked.

"No, but Dad said he arrived a couple of days ago. He's a white-haired old man."

"Great," Joseph said. "They send us some old guy who'll probably have a heart attack if we try anything fun. Why can't we get a native teacher?"

"There aren't that many yet. Finish high school, go to college, and you could come back and be one," Simon suggested.

"No, thanks. You're the smart one. And I don't like

the city," Joseph said. Simon nodded in agreement. They both had seen high school graduates like Mary Paniak and Robert Henry go away to college, beaming with excitement and dreams, only to return a few months later, beaten and discouraged. And then there were those like Andrew Jacob, Joseph's cousin, who went away and never came back, too much like a kass'aq to fit in.

And then there was Joseph's uncle Frank—Junior, the family called him—the youngest of Grandfather's four children. He had gone away to art school, showing promising talent. The last anyone had heard, he was living in Anchorage on the streets. Junior would have done fine if he had stayed in Napamiut. He could have made masks and carvings to sell on consignment in town, as Joseph's mother did with the hats and mukluks she sewed. Instead, he had tried to make it the kass'aq way, and the kass'aq way had ruined him.

Joseph and Simon reached the community center and edged open the heavy door. The room was already hot with bodies that carried the familiar smells of smoked fish and Pinesol into the meeting with them. Joseph scanned the crowd. Was Grandfather there? Old women squatted against the walls, talking softly to one another. There was Mary Paniak, bouncing a chubby-cheeked baby on her hip. Beside her stood Elena's mom, Gertrude Nicholai, her tongue flapping at old Nastasia Paniak. Every nod of agreement from Nastasia revealed her triple chin.

The men were seated for business in a circle of folding chairs. Simon's father, Paul Andrew, sat stiffly beside

15

Alexie John. Alexie's shoulders were squared under his flannel shirt, his eyes blinked behind thick-rimmed glasses. To the other side of the city manager sat Elena's father, Robert, the stout storekeeper, whose face was animated with some story, punctuated by an occasional thrust of his stubby finger.

A group of small children, mostly girls, giggled in one corner. And there, in the other corner, sat Grandfather. He was listening to Wasillie Sam, the village postmaster, who stood beside him, relating some tale with lively eyes and gestures. Grandfather did not look in their direction until Joseph and Simon slid to the dusty floor near the door. Joseph breathed a momentary sigh of relief as he sat.

Up front, a sandy-haired brownshirt stood, shifting his slight weight back and forth, his wire-rimmed eyes on Alexie John, who rose to stand beside him. A dark-haired trooper with a fierce mustache leaned tall and sturdy against the wall a few yards from his companion and surveyed the crowd.

Alexie cleared his throat loudly, and the voices fell silent, except for the children in the corner. He was round and pudgy, like an overgrown schoolboy, but his voice was firm and resolute as he addressed the people. "Troopers Rothman and Smith are paying us a visit today. We will listen to what they tell us about the fish, and then they will listen to what we tell them. First, Trooper Rothman." Having issued the order, Alexie stepped back and folded his arms across his chest.

"Well, as most of you know," the sandy-haired brown-shirt began, "we have had to institute an emergency

16

closure on the subsistence harvest of silver salmon. The runs have been declining in recent years and show no sign of recovering. The return this year has been especially poor. We must leave the fish to spawn or eventually none will return."

Joseph glanced across the room at his grandfather. His face had lost animation; he stared blankly at the brownshirt who spoke this news of a closure. Then his face dropped and he shook his head. Joseph looked away.

The trooper looked around the room. "I—We—realize the hardship that this places on some of you, on many of you. But we really have no choice. We must ask you to respect the closure."

The faces stared steadily at the white man, who flushed and shifted. After a moment of silence, Peter Angaiak, one of the elders, rose unsteadily from his chair to speak. He began slowly, his voice rising and falling in a melody of Yup'ik, his sun-darkened face growing more agitated as he spoke. His bushy eyebrows lifted and fell with the force of his words. Then he sat as slowly as he had stood and waited while his daughter Florence, a young bilingual aide at the grade school, translated.

"He says," the young woman began, " 'who at your agency is so full of knowledge of our rivers that he can make this decision? Our people have lived here and fished these rivers for hundreds of years. We know our rivers and our fish. Yes, there may be periods of low harvest. But the fish always return.' "

"Well, that may have been true in the past," the

brownshirt replied. "But now you're using longer gill nets and bigger motorboats. You've harvested more fish than ever using new technology. We have to manage the resource or it will be lost."

"You say we're using faster boats and better nets," Robert Nicholai, the storekeeper, addressed the trooper in English. "But if that were the only factor, our fish racks would fill up faster than ever. Look around you. We have been fishing hard with our faster boats and our better nets, and our racks are only half-full. There must be a bigger problem."

The fair-headed brownshirt nodded. "Yes, it's a bigger problem. Japanese and Russian boats make incidental catches on the high seas. They're not fishing for salmon; they're bottom fishing with trawlers for cod and pollock. But salmon—some of them bound for these rivers—get caught in their nets just the same. They never return to spawn. It's a downward spiral."

The trooper coughed lightly. Joseph imagined his throat was dry with the rising heat of the room. Then the trooper continued. "Fishermen in other parts of the state intercept salmon bound for the Kuskokwim and its tributaries, like Long River here. But how can we stop them? They're trying to make a living just like you."

Joseph shifted where he sat, cross-legged, on the dusty floor. Objections pounded in his head. If the kass'aqs had never come . . . If we could return to the old ways . . . our lives were simpler then. . . . Leave us alone and let us work it out. Though he knew he was not old enough to voice his concerns in this forum, Joseph longed to speak his mind. But he also knew that, even if he could speak out, his words would spew forth in quick anger, as they did so often with his mother, and that would be a disgrace to everyone.

Joseph's rumbling thoughts were interrupted as Alexie John stepped forward and spoke, his voice steady but commanding. "We're not talking about making money here. Everything to you is in dollars and cents. This is our way of life, our sustenance, our heritage. Our people have used the salmon, and used it wisely, for thousands of years. We have dried its flesh, made raincoats from its skin, boiled its head for soup. How can we, who know it so well, trust you outsiders to manage it for us?"

Joseph nodded in agreement, proud of Alexie for standing up and speaking these thoughts on behalf of them all.

"Trust? I'll tell you about trust." The tall brownshirt, Trooper Smith, who had been leaning against the wall, strode forward and looked down at Alexie John. He spoke with force, staring directly at Alexie and then challenging the circle of villagers with his flashing eyes. "Our closure hasn't been in effect for even twenty-four hours, and we see one of your boats from the air, harvesting fish just as you please. You people can't be trusted to follow a simple guideline!" The last words were an angry yell, like a father void of patience with his erring children.

We only got three fish, Joseph thought, his own anger seething toward the surface. And just try to find out who we were, he added defiantly to himself. He wished he could speak the words aloud, though to reveal these thoughts would be the ultimate foolishness.

19

Alexie John stood firm, his eyes locking in kass'aq manner with the trooper. "We want you to reconsider the guidelines. These are a frustrated people." His hand swept before the crowd. "They are tired of being told what to do by people who don't know or understand them, by people who could care less." Several heads nodded, including Joseph's.

"You do have a representative on the state game board," the smaller trooper replied in a nervous voice.

"One representative, selected by the governor. How can he speak for all Yup'ik people? And who hears him?" Alexie challenged.

People stood to speak more quickly now, reiterating what Alexie and the others had said, complaining about the lack of true voice in decision making. It began to look as though the meeting might drag on so long that the troopers would return to Bainbridge without investigating the fishing violation any further. At least Joseph hoped so.

The fury of the moment built, and the room became engulfed with heat. It's like screaming into the wind, Joseph thought angrily. We'll all say our bit and feel a little better, and these brownshirts will fly off in their Cessna, back to their offices where they'll make more stupid decisions without considering us.

Then it hit him: the Cessna. Joseph pictured it alone on the runway, the offensive vehicle used to spot his misdeed, tied down against the force of the wind. Maybe there was a way to get the attention of these kass'aqs, or if not that, at least the satisfaction of revenge.

Joseph nudged Simon and waved a silent good-bye

even as the heated voices continued. Simon started to get up, his brow wrinkled and his eyes puzzled, but Joseph shook his head. He rose and headed—inconspicuously, he hoped—out the door.

The airstrip sat at the west end of the village, on a hillock of firm ground bolstered with gravel brought in on the barge. Joseph strode firmly on the boardwalks, past young boys shooting baskets on an outdoor court made of planks, practicing layups like those they had seen on TV.

He forced himself not to run, but he wanted to reach the airstrip in time. Past Nicholai's store, past the tiny Russian church with its onion-domed steeple, past old Balassa Andrews, who sat on her steps and waved. Joseph held up a hand in acknowledgment, but didn't slow his pace or turn his head.

Finally the boardwalk turned to a single, dead-end path, bordered by three-foot-high scrub willow bushes. The westerly wind whipped Joseph's face, making his eyes water. At least the drizzle had stopped.

The Cessna, which had seemed tiny from the edge of the village, grew to life-size as Joseph neared the runway. Its wings flexed and shivered in the wind. The troopers had brought it to a stop at the village end of the runway, and there it waited, nose pointed in the direction of Bainbridge, some thirty miles away.

Joseph ducked behind a row of bright blue fifty-five-gallon oil drums on the left side of the runway, just behind the tail of the aircraft. The runway was deserted, of course. People only gathered there if a mail plane was due in, which was around noon each weekday.

21

Still, Joseph wanted to be cautious. He peered over the top of one blue drum and scanned the tundra surrounding the airstrip. He listened. One of the drums sounded a loud thump, its side flexing with the force of the wind. No children played in the tall grass, no women chattered as they picked August cranberries. Good. He ventured out in a crouched run toward the Cessna.

His anger transformed itself to a thrill of pounding heart and heightened senses as he reached the plane. Quickly, he told himself. The meeting could have ended; the troopers could be on the boardwalk, heading back to the airport now. Pulling his jackknife from his pocket, he made three sharp, deep slashes in each airplane tire, starting with the two under the wings, then moving to the single tire beneath the tail.

Joseph walked back toward the front of the aircraft. It appeared unchanged. Eager to see results, Joseph pushed with the weight of his whole body on the fender of the right front tire. It gave way under his weight, and the plane resettled lopsidedly, its right wing dipping toward the runway. Yes! If the brownshirts didn't get it at the meeting, they would know when they saw their plane: Stay away. Don't fly over the river looking for kids and their grandfathers who just need a few more fish for the winter.

A crooked smile crossed Joseph's face as he ran back to the barrels. He ducked again for a moment, caught his breath, and finished his plan. It was important not to get caught on the path back to the village, but if he wandered too far out, his return would be prolonged and his presence out on the open tundra might draw attention.

He decided to walk back on the tundra but stick close to the airport path. He listened for voices as he made his way through the tall grasses alongside the willows, but the only sound he heard was the squish of cold tundra water through his sneakers.

Among the gnarled bushes near the airstrip, though, someone else was listening closely and had been ever since he heard the footfall of Joseph's sneakers as they brought him to the plane. The new schoolteacher, prematurely white hair framing his forty-something face, had looked up from the hillock where he was gathering cranberries.

He had puzzled a moment over what the tall native boy with the wavy hair might be doing at the wheels of an aircraft. He didn't know any of the village young people yet; tomorrow would be the first day of school, and he would begin the process of getting acquainted then, a process that he knew from twelve years of experience teaching in villages along the Yukon River to the north would take a long, long time.

But if he did not know the boy, he did know the act he had committed once he saw one wing tip hanging low toward the runway. From within an instinct rose: Confront the offender and bring him to justice. But reason stifled the instinct. He was new in the village, an outsider whose status could be precarious for many years, should he choose to stay that long.

Better to wait. He took a final, hard look at the boy's face, then ducked back behind the hillock to resume the tedious task of filling his empty margarine tub with cranberries. He breathed in the smell of minty tundra tea and focused on the delicately balanced life before him—spongy brown sphagnum moss, lacy white reindeer moss, curled yellow lichens, oily leaves of lingonberry hugging close to the soggy ground.

He couldn't upset his own delicate relationship with the villagers—not just yet, not until he knew more, the schoolteacher thought. He would wait.

THREE

THE VILLAGE HAD SPRUNG TO LIFE by the time Joseph reached the boardwalk. Clearly, the meeting had been dismissed. Women in bright, hooded *qaspeqs* and sweatshirts, men in flannels and jeans, and children in overalls and sneakers were streaming from the community center. Some walked alone, looking thoughtful, but most were in groups of two or three, talking earnestly in Yup'ik.

Joseph overheard snatches of conversation: "Laws made in Juneau . . ." "Dogs hungry this winter . . ." "Not much we can do now . . ." "Maybe next summer." He tried to look nonchalant as he made his way back to the community center to see if Simon was still nearby. Once inside, though, he felt giddy with the relief of not being caught and with the satisfaction of taking action, and he had to hold back a grin.

Simon was still at the community center, racking up balls at a pool table in the back.

"Where'd you go in such a hurry?" he asked Joseph.

"No place in particular," Joseph replied, but a grin slipped out when he opened his mouth.

"You're up to something."

"Shhhh!" Joseph's eyes spoke along with his lips as he

25

drew closer to his friend. Joseph eyed a group of young men who were huddled not far from the pool table. They were debating the fishing restrictions among themselves, with angry words about kass'aq interference and the need for local control. No one had so much as glanced at Joseph and Simon.

"You'll find out soon enough, but I'm not telling you myself, just in case anyone asks any questions," Joseph said, his dark eyes dancing with mischief.

Simon pushed up his glasses and grabbed a pool cue off the rack on the wall. "OK, I hear you. Challenge you to a game."

They played for an hour, with Simon winning every round. He made long, calculated shots with an inner energy that Joseph didn't understand. Simon could be so quiet and unassuming—the model preacher's kid— but at pool he was all slam and kill. "It's a good thing you're my friend," Joseph said as they replaced the cues after the final trouncing. "Otherwise I'd be mad!" He grinned and slapped Simon on the back. "See you later."

The satisfaction of sabotaging the plane returned to the front of Joseph's mind as he headed home for dinner, unafraid and in control. Only when he reached for the door of the house did he remember the problem of the fish and Grandfather. The euphoria slid off, like snow from a roof in the spring.

His mother, awake now, stood at the table kneading dough, while grease sizzled in a skillet for the fry bread she was forming. Without looking up, she said, "Your grandfather called on the CB. He wants you to have supper with him tonight. I tried to get him to come here instead, but he was insistent."

Anna Benchley's voice was low and calm, forming the Yup'ik words with care as she pushed the dough up and out with the heels of her hands. A smudge of flour lightened her cheek, and a loose band held back her long, straight hair. She looked up at Joseph, and her eyes signaled a question. Joseph looked away. "OK, I'm going then," he said.

"You want to wait for fry bread. . . ?" Joseph heard the question begin, but turned back out and slammed the door before his mother could finish.

He pulled the bucket from behind coats and boots on the porch and hunted for a plastic lid to cover the fish. He found one, snapped it in place, and set off down the boardwalk.

As he walked, Joseph looked back at the tiny kitchen window. Inside, his mother stopped kneading a moment and caught his eye. Perhaps she wondered what was in the bucket, but he knew she would never ask. She pulled back a strand of hair from her face and began to shape flat fry bread circles.

Joseph looked toward his destination. Frank Paul's house was little more than a shack. The paint had long ago worn off the weather-beaten outer walls, and it was not much bigger than the steam bath in back—just taller. But Joseph knew this location past the far end of the village kept his grandfather's life quiet and peaceful. His home was fifty yards from the last cluster of houses, and the boardwalk ended ten yards past his front door. From there, the winding river, the waving

27

grasses, and the spongy tundra stretched to the eastern horizon.

Joseph went in without knocking and set his bucket on the plank floor. His grandfather sat at the tiny Formica table sharpening his *uluaq,* the crescent-shaped fish-cutting tool with a bone handle that had served him for many seasons. "We must not waste them," he said quietly, without looking up. Joseph nodded.

They went outside, Joseph lugging the bucket. His grandfather motioned for him to pull the fish-cutting table, made of rough planks, toward the river. They stood beside it, knee-high in the tall grasses. It was getting darker now, and the sky had turned a cool slate color of evening. In the west, the setting sun shone beneath a layer of clouds, casting a rich glow of angled light on the grasses, the river, and the two outlaw fishermen.

Joseph laid the first fish on the table and watched the old man use the sharp blade to slice off the head and to open the belly. Joseph threw the head and guts into the bucket. His grandfather maneuvered the *uluaq* with quick flicks of the wrist up the length of the fish, carving out nearly fleshless ribs and spine, leaving the side meat hanging at the tail. Then he cut rhythmic slices that gaped open like grins all along the length of the fish, one-half inch apart, exposing the flesh to plenty of air so it could dry. Silence hung thick about the two, wrapping them in centuries of tradition, the younger watching each nuance of movement in his elder. This was normally women's work, but the men learned it, too, so they could survive alone if need be. Joseph's grandfather had lived alone, cutting his own fish, since the death of his wife nearly seven years earlier.

Grandfather lifted the completed fish, its two carefully fashioned fillets still joined at the tail, and nodded his head toward the other two yet in the bucket. Joseph picked them up; they weighed heavy in each hand like weights on a scale, about eight pounds apiece. He handed first one and then the other to his grandfather, watching the deft movements, wondering if he could replicate them.

When all three fish had been cleaned and cut, Joseph hung two over one arm and grasped the other in his free hand. The old man led the way to the smokehouse, a tiny wooden shed beside the steam bath. Normally the fish would have dried on racks in the open air for a week or so, but they could not risk drawing attention to their catch by leaving it out. The flies were all but gone now, so the cool air of the smokehouse could dry them safely, though more slowly than if they were hung outside. As the smokehouse door creaked open, the smell of wood, smoke, and dried fish filled their nostrils, cool and comforting in the darkness.

They hung the freshly cut fish to the side, away from the other salmon, which had recently been cold-smoked and were ready for winter storage. Even now, Joseph looked ahead to frosty winter nights, when the snow would swirl around Grandfather's tiny house, and he and the old man would sit together inside, chewing the dry fish, savoring its smoky taste, and remembering the promise of summer and life on the river. After months had gone by, would the taste be spoiled by the memory of his deception, Joseph wondered.

Not a word had passed between Joseph and his grandfather concerning the illegal status of these fish or the meeting this afternoon. Joseph knew his grandfather had not seen him come into the meeting, but in his hurry to get to the airstrip, he had forgotten to check for Grandfather's watchful eye as he left the community center. How much did he guess?

The silence between them grew like a drift of snow built by a cold winter wind.

"Hungry?" Grandfather asked Joseph at last. The sunset had painted the sky in streaks of orange and pink. They entered the house, where darkness now hung in the corners of the room. Joseph nodded his reply: He was hungry. He made his way to the shallow washbasin to clean his hands in the soapy water. He glanced at his image in the framed mirror above the basin—the dark wavy hair, round eyes, sharp nose—and felt a wave of dissatisfaction overwhelm him.

There was so much left unsaid between them. What did Grandfather think, now that he knew they had taken the fish illegally? Surely he believed, like Joseph, that their rights to the river and their winter need for fish took precedence over the kass'aq regulation.

But Joseph knew his grandfather had every right to be angry that his grandson hadn't told him about the closure. Joseph pondered as he watched the old man take a pot of leftover stew from his small refrigerator and set it on the flat-topped oil stove. He could pretend he hadn't known about the closure, but his grandfather wasn't easy to deceive. His eyes could bore right into a person's mind. Wondering about it all was beginning to gnaw at Joseph. A person could hide forever behind the traditional cloak of silence, but Joseph was beginning to wish his grandfather would say something so he would know where he stood.

Joseph considered whether to speak and what to say. His grandfather stood at the stove stirring the stew. Joseph didn't want to bring up the meeting, or the troopers, or anything that might connect him with the plane. He had lost the proud feeling of satisfaction that had swelled within him when he slashed the tires, and he couldn't seem to will it back. He took a seat in one of the bent-metal chairs.

"School starts tomorrow, Ap'a." Joseph decided to break the silence with a completely different topic.

"Iii. No more fishing," Grandfather replied, his dark eyes locking with Joseph's. Joseph looked down.

"There's a new teacher," Joseph said.

"So I hear—a white-haired man like me," Grandfather said.

"Humph! Not like you, I'm sure. Another kass'aq." Joseph's tone was harsh.

"Like your father, Joseph," Grandfather said gently, setting a bowl of stew in front of his grandson.

The words stung. After all these years, the deep wound of a kass'aq father who had left his family to live Outside rose to the surface and burned there. Hot steam from the stew met his lowered face, and his eyes watered. Joseph said nothing, but reached for his spoon and shoveled ferociously at the stew, feeling more empty even as he filled his stomach.

They ate, wrapped once again in murky silence, and

then Grandfather switched on the soft light of a table lamp and poured them each a cup of hot tea from the kettle bubbling on the stove.

"You must light the steam bath, Joseph," he said. "My bones are feeling old and tired tonight."

Joseph nodded and rose from the table. Cool evening air greeted him as he stepped outside. The wind had blown away all but a few wisps of cloud from the inky sky. He loaded his arms with driftwood from the pile beside the steam bath and ducked low, first through the tiny dressing room and then into the main section where the half-barrel stove sat in a pile of rocks. He stuffed the stove with the wood, then went back out to pull some dry tundra grass for kindling. Returning to the steam room, he tucked the grass beneath the wood and lit a match.

Joseph watched the flame leap from its tiny start to engulf a driftwood limb. The dry wood sparked and snapped, releasing energy that had been stored up for decades, or perhaps centuries. This driftwood had come from trees far up the river, trees that had battled for survival at the edge of the permafrost. Joseph knew they grew only a few inches a year, and their struggle for life had probably ended in an instant during a raging spring flood. These flames would be the last glow, the final release, after a long battle against the harsh elements.

Sure now that the fire was well underway, Joseph returned inside to get his grandfather. They listened to the CB chatter for ten minutes, giving the heat a chance to build inside the steam bath. Gertrude Nicholai was looking for her nephew; he was needed for hauling water. Florence Angaiak and her cousin were planning a boat trip to Bainbridge the next day to get groceries. And two men—Wasillie Sam and Peter Angaiak—were discussing how someone had slit the tires of the troopers' Cessna and how the troopers now were staying the night in the school gym, until a mechanic from Bainbridge could bring new tires tomorrow.

Grandfather lifted a gray eyebrow at this last bit of news, and Joseph did his best to maintain his face without expression. He waited for a discussion to ensue. The old man looked small and shriveled, slumped in the kitchen chair. The indoor light chased its way into each of his wrinkles. It seemed only yesterday that his grandfather had been strong and invincible.

The CB chatter continued. At last, Grandfather rose and gathered the towels. Joseph dipped a bucket 'of water from the huge plastic trash-can-turned-water-container in the corner, and he grabbed the soap from the basin. Side by side, in silence still, Joseph and his grandfather headed for the steam bath. Now the stovepipe glowed red against the night sky, and sparks shot from the chimney.

Hunched over in the pitch-black of the dressing room, they disrobed, feeling about for protruding nails on which they hung their clothes. Joseph heard his grandfather move slowly in the darkness and pull the peg handle of the steam-bath door. As Grandfather entered the steam room, Joseph behind him, a blast of hot, dry air greeted them.

Only the faintest glow of light came from the stove, where the wood crackled and sang with the burning.

Joseph and his grandfather settled on the floor, leaning against opposite walls, two silhouettes in the almost-darkness. As Grandfather ladled the water onto rocks around the stove, it spit and sizzled, and the room filled with steam. Joseph's nostrils stung with the heat of the moist air, but it warmed his lungs and brought cleansing sweat to his pores. His muscles relaxed. He hadn't realized how much tension he had built up.

As the steam settled and the air took on a delicious warmth, Grandfather began to speak. "Today there was much difficulty among our people." Joseph nodded slowly, and the old man continued. "I saw you leave the meeting, so I know you felt it, too."

He paused a moment, drawing a deep breath of moist air into his lungs. "And now I understand your rush to return from fishing." There was a long silence, with only the crackling of the fire to fill their ears. Joseph waited for the reprimand. Even if Grandfather agreed that they had a right to fish once more despite the closure, there still was the fact that Joseph had not told him they were fishing illegally.

But when Grandfather opened his mouth again to speak, it was not a reprimand but his lilting storytelling voice, soothing and melodious, like a flock of sandhill cranes, that greeted Joseph.

"When I was young, they told the story of a young man named Teparlluar, who lived on the coast and went down to the sea ice one spring for hunting. He took grass for a blanket and his kayak. When he reached the ocean, darkness was falling fast, so he set up the grass mat and slept.

"He did not wake until it was morning and the sun was shining brightly. A tiny bird perched on his grass mat and spoke to him, telling him that the wind had shifted and spring had come. Sure enough, when he stood and looked around, he saw that his bed was on a sheet of drift ice, floating out in the sea somewhere.

"This man, though a hunter, was frightened at the feeling of drifting alone in the ocean. He looked around for his harpoon, realizing that he would need it to get food. But all he saw was his skin kayak. As the days went by, Teparlluar grew so hungry that he had to chew his kayak for nourishment, one piece at a time."

Grandfather paused. His eyes took on a faraway look, as if gazing beyond the darkness to the scene he described. Then he poured more water on the rocks. The steam burned even hotter now, and Joseph hung his head low to breathe. When the air cleared, he lifted his head. Grandfather cleared his throat and continued.

"Finally one morning Teparlluar woke up and saw that the scenery had changed. Instead of the endless stretches of water and floating ice chunks, he saw mountains all around him. The piece of ice that had become his home had finally washed up onto land. He looked closer and saw a village in the distance. Without thinking, he got up and walked quickly toward it.

"When he reached the village, Teparlluar immediately noticed something strange. The women were all *qulugteq*—all hunched over. So he asked one of the men why this was so, and the man replied that when a woman was pregnant and ready to give birth, the men would cut them open with their knives and remove the babies. That was why the women were all hunched over."

Grandfather coughed in the cooling air. He dipped and poured more water. Joseph held his head up this time and watched the steam rise from the sizzling rocks. Then his grandfather went on with the story.

"It just so happened that this man Teparlluar spoke with had a wife who was just about to have her first baby. So Teparlluar offered to teach them a new way to deliver the baby, like the women did in his village. When the woman's time came, Teparlluar did exactly that, and the people of the village were pleased. This man had brought a good change to their old ways, and now their women no longer had to be *qulugteq*.

"That wasn't the only change that Teparlluar brought to the village. You see, these people knew nothing about washing clothes. One day Teparlluar washed his hat and hung it out to dry. The people were amazed that his hat looked like a brand-new one. He explained to them about washing, and soon all the people's clothes were looking like brand-new."

Grandfather's voice deepened, and Joseph saw a frown cross his face in the firelight. "Teparlluar was quite content to be helping these people. Then one day he heard from some children that a group of the men were angry about his new ways of doing things and were planning to kill him.

"So he went to his friend, the very first man he had met in that place, and asked for his help in escaping. The man gave him a kayak and one oar. He tied the oar to Teparlluar's arm so he wouldn't lose it even if he got tired. Then Teparlluar hid in the tall grasses until night-fall. He heard men walking around, saying, 'Where is Teparlluar?' When the voices stopped, he sneaked over to the ocean and set off. After many days and nights, he finally came back to his village. . . ."

The old man's voice trailed off, and the only sound left was the crackling of the wood as it burned. The searing heat had dissipated, and Joseph felt enveloped by the comforting warmth that remained. He closed his eyes and leaned back against the rough wall, now cool enough to touch.

He could feel the pain of the young man, pursued by those he tried to help, and he wondered at the anger of the villagers, so intense against the stranger. His eyes still closed, Joseph heard his grandfather speak once more:

"Teparlluar never forgot how those people hated him for bringing change to that place."

Bringing change to that place . . . those people hated him. The words swirled in the darkness of Joseph's thoughts. For a moment he felt light-headed, and disoriented thoughts stumbled into one another.

Joseph forced his eyes open. There sat Grandfather, running slippery soap over his sweaty skin. Joseph reached for another bar of soap and made his own thin lather, then rinsed himself with a splash of warm water from the bucket.

When they left the steam bath, feeling warm and tired, Joseph saw that the sky had cleared completely, leaving hundreds of stars to swirl above them in the black of night. He carried the bucket and soap to the doorstep for his grandfather. Standing in the darkness beside the front door, he found words for his question.

"Grandfather, why did they hate him?"

There was a moment of silence, followed by his grandfather's reply. "There are many sides, like edges of a sharp stone, to the anger that builds within us. We use it to chase our enemies, sometimes without knowing who they are."

The old man's face was solemn. With a slight nod, he stepped up and into his porch. Joseph walked slowly down the boardwalk to his own house, puzzling.

Later that night, nestled into the bunk above Sam, Joseph saw himself in a dream, floating adrift on a pack of cold sea ice. Suddenly he was on land again, panting and chasing after a stranger in a brown shirt. Faster and faster he ran, leaving the others behind, until it was just him and the stranger. As he reached out to grab the stranger by the collar, the man turned, and Joseph saw with horror that the face was his own, his eyes dark and wide with fear. He woke with a start. Then he lay staring into the empty darkness for what seemed like a very long time.

FOUR

WHEN JOSEPH PUSHED HIMSELF OUT OF BED the next morning, the dream images were still vivid in his mind. He shuddered at the memory of chasing and being chased, but as he began to dress, the images and the feeling of horror faded.

He pulled on a pair of old jeans with a new T-shirt, purchased for this day when his family had traveled by boat to Bainbridge two weeks ago, with him at the motor and Grandfather beside him as they made their way through the maze of winding sloughs and rivers.

Today the Benchleys' house was alive with activity.

"That one's mine," Dora shrieked. Joseph looked around the corner of the bedroom and saw his sister snatch a bright fuchsia sweatshirt from Elsie's hands. Elsie's eyes narrowed and she let out a screech.

"Mom!" Elsie yelled for help even as she took matters, and the sweatshirt, into her own hands. A tug-of-war ensued.

"*Akleng.*" Anna spoke firmly as she reached for the new shirt. "You'll tear it. This one is Dora's." The girls exchanged a scowl, and Elsie released her grip, but not before Dora stuck out her tongue at her younger sister.

"You think you're so special to be starting seventh

39

grade. I'm just two years behind you," Elsie said under her breath.

Joseph shook his head and reached for his socks. Good thing Sam was way too small to go after his clothes. Joseph knew that if his little brother were even remotely close to his size, he would like nothing better than to adopt Joseph's whole wardrobe, limited as it was. Sam was a lot like a puppy that curls up to sleep on a pile of your clothes because he just can't get enough of you. His admiration was flattering at times, but it could get annoying real fast.

Today Sam had his mind on other things. As he put on his shoes, Joseph heard his brother whine.

"I can't sit all day in class. Why can't I just stay half a day, like in kindergarten?" Sam complained.

"Because," his mother answered as she reached for a striped shirt flung to the floor the night before.

Joseph peered through the heavy bedroom curtains and saw a day bright with sunshine and blue skies. Sam had a point. They'd have to spend the first sunny day in a week cramped up inside a nearly windowless building. And they'd have to speak English, at least to the teachers.

Even so, he didn't want to be late on the first day. He stepped over to the table and quickly spread some jam on a thick, flat pilot cracker. Still chewing, he surveyed himself in the mirror above the washbasin. His wavy hair went in all directions, and he wet a brush to tame it. The waves settled back, slick and straight, with the help of the water, and for a moment his hair resembled that of any other fourteen-year-old Yup'ik male—black,

40

shiny, and straight. He frowned at the mirror. His face was still too long and thin, with a protruding nose. And the waves would bounce back as his hair dried. Joseph shook his head in disgust, grabbed his backpack, and headed for the door.

"Take your brother with you," his mother instructed. She sat at the table, her face placid and still not quite awake as she sipped a mug of steaming tea.

"He knows the way, Mom. It's not like he hasn't lived here his whole life." Joseph shifted with impatience, his hand on the doorknob.

"Joseph." Her tone was curt and her gaze intense. She wasn't going to let it rest.

"OK, OK, but only if he comes right now. Sam!" Joseph yelled in the direction of the bedroom, where he could hear his little brother fumbling around with the dresser drawers.

"Right now, Sam. I'm counting to three." Joseph shot his mother a firm look. "One . . . two . . ."

Sam came running from the bedroom, his shirt mis-buttoned and his hair uncombed. Joseph had to grin in spite of himself. Had he looked like this, dashing off to school at six years old? Everything was so simple then— no one really cared or thought too much about things. He reached down to tousle Sam's already mussed hair. Then he knelt to rebutton his brother's shirt.

"You look a mess," he chided. "Now, let's go." The pair bounded out the door, their feet hitting the board-walk with authority.

"Oh, no," Joseph said softly, turning to Sam. "Look at that."

There stood Elena Nicholai, at the junction of her boardwalk and the main one, smiling coyly at Joseph and his brother. Her thick black hair was primped and curled. Her eyes looked tiny under heavy shadow and liner. She was only starting ninth grade like Joseph, but by the way her face was made up, she could have passed for a soap opera heroine on her way to her third wedding.

"Isn't it a gorgeous day? I can't wait to finally be at the high school. And where have you been lately, Joseph? I've hardly seen you around." Elena shot the questions at him as she nudged in beside Joseph and Sam on the boardwalk. Joseph picked up the pace, but she kept right up. He was glad Sam was there now; otherwise, her hot breath and grating voice would be right in his face.

Elena didn't wait for any answers—it seemed to Joseph that she never did. Instead, she plunged ahead with more commentary. "Say, did you hear what happened yesterday? Well, you know the troopers came out—Fish and Game, that is. Seems there was a big meeting at the community center—some hubbub over fishing restrictions or closed seasons or something like that. I didn't go to the meeting, of course. Who cares about regulations or fish? Ugh."

She paused to catch her breath. Joseph was walking extrafast now, shaking his head. Elena was probably the only Eskimo in the world who didn't like fish. She was an embarrassment any way you looked at it.

"My soap opera was on then—you know, the one where Ted and Donna just got a divorce, but now

42

Donna's twin sister mysteriously disappeared, and it looks like Ted murdered her, thinking it was Donna." Elena's face shone with enthusiasm.

"Anyway . . ." Joseph growled.

"Anyway, after that meeting, when the troopers went to leave, you'll never guess." Joseph wasn't about to. He was anxious to hear what everyone else knew about the plane, though, so he looked in Elena's direction.

"What happened?" he asked.

"Well, nothing really happened then. I mean, I guess it happened during the meeting. Did you say you were there?"

I haven't said a thing, Joseph thought to himself. He nodded, hoping he looked casual about the topic, and Elena continued.

"Someone slashed the tires on the troopers' plane. It's still sitting there on the runway. Of course, they had to spend the night. No one can figure who did it, or at least they aren't saying if they know. Funny thing, my dad said. They didn't seem to be looking around at all last night to investigate."

"Maybe they figured they had it coming," Joseph mumbled. They had reached the front steps of the pale yellow grade school building where he, Elena, and nine classmates, more or less, had gone through eight years of kass'aq education together.

"Bye, guy," Joseph said to Sam. He patted his back, and Sam looked up with a grin. Then he turned, and Joseph watched him charge up the steps to begin his first day of first grade.

With Sam gone, Elena sidled up close beside Joseph,

as if the boardwalk were only a foot wide. "We're gonna be late," he admonished, and took off running. Elena's clacky new shoes were no match for his sneakers, so Joseph captured a few minutes of exhilarated running alone before he reached the spiky metal high school steps. Joseph glanced over his shoulder as he bounded up the stairs. Elena had given up her pursuit and slowed to walk beside her friend Elsie Charles. Even from this distance, Joseph could see Elena's tongue wagging. He turned around and opened the heavy door.

Unlike the grade school, which had been in the center of the village for thirty years, the high school was a new building in the northwest corner, not far from the runway and the winding river. It sat high off the tundra on fancy pilings that had cooling systems to deter the melting of permafrost beneath the spongy ground. Without these, the thawing ground would cause the building to shift and settle like a cockeyed boat thrust up onto the beach by the tide.

The high school roof slanted asymmetrically to a modern-looking, off-center peak. The building still smelled like new plastic, Joseph noticed as he went in, even though it had been open for three years now. This was far from Joseph's first time in the building. Basketball and wrestling tournaments—big village events in the winter—were held here on a regular basis. Now, for four years, it would be his school.

Big deal, Joseph told himself. But he remembered the choice his mother had to make as a teenager—go to a boarding school in Bainbridge, or quit after eighth grade. Anna had endured the Bainbridge school for a year, living uncomfortably in a kass'aq boarding home.

But after a carefree summer of cutting fish with her family and neighbors, the homesickness she suffered upon returning to school in the fall grew too strong. Besides, Anna's mother had contracted fish poisoning when she cut her hand putting up the last of the silver salmon, and Anna was needed at home.

So, only a week into her sophomore year, Anna had dropped out of school. And her life hadn't been so bad, Joseph thought. Her best friend Hannah had come home a few weeks later to help her older sister with her new baby, and as far as Joseph knew, neither one had given any thought to going back. He didn't see why his mom wouldn't let him quit school. She always had a little speech about how she wanted him to have all the opportunities of a high school education.

So even though he hated school, Joseph had stuck it out so far. But only because the village had its own high school now. He knew he couldn't tolerate school if he had to attend one in a half-kass'aq town.

"Hey, what's the hurry?" Simon's voice broke through Joseph's thoughts. He was waiting in the entryway, his straight black hair neatly combed back and a button-down shirt tucked into his jeans.

"Just running away from my friend Elena," Joseph said under his breath, and Simon grinned.

"I get it. Did your ears fall off yet?"

"That's why I thought I'd better run."

The two boys made their way to the gym, where the other students were gathering, and settled themselves on the floor behind most of their thirty-nine schoolmates to wait for introductions and directions for the day.

"Hey, Joseph. I heard something interesting last

night. Something about the tires of a plane being slashed," Simon said in a low voice, pushing up his glasses as he spoke.

"Yeah, I heard that, too."

"Well, I was just wondering—"

"Shhhh! Mr. Kingston's trying to get our attention," Joseph interrupted. His dark eyes were firm and direct, signaling silence to Simon.

The short, balding kass'aq principal, Mr. Kingston, gave an animated welcome, with his smiley, curly-haired wife at his side. He even told two jokes, at which all the students, including Joseph, groaned. The Kingstons were all right, from what Joseph knew. They had been in Napamiut for five years, and they minded their own business.

But you never knew about the new ones. Mr. Kingston motioned for a white-haired man with wire-rimmed glasses to come to the front. "I'd like you all to welcome Mr. Townsend, our new English and social studies teacher, to Napamiut High School," the principal said with enthusiasm. He brought his hands together in a loud clap, and a smattering of the students followed his lead. Joseph did not.

Instead, he eyed the new teacher carefully. He didn't look old enough to have white hair. His skin was barely wrinkled, and he stood tall and strong. But his eyes were as cool as glacier ice, and he didn't smile. A formidable foe, Joseph thought. He squared himself for the challenge. Joseph had a reputation for making new teachers squirm.

Once Mr. Kingston had given his instructions for the

day, Napamiut High School's small student body headed for the main part of the building, which was one huge room partitioned off into three separate classrooms. For Simon and Joseph, pre-algebra was first, with Mrs. Kingston in charge. She led them through a series of review problems. Next was biology, again with Mrs. Kingston, but in a different section of the partitioned room with several older students, since science was a mixed-grade elective. Faint scents of formaldehyde and vinegar hovered in the air as she explained rules for lab use and passed out textbooks.

After science, Joseph and Simon returned to the area where they had earlier done math problems. This time, it was designated for ninth-grade English. The new teacher sat at his desk, looking over his roll book for the class. The bell rang, a short, punctuated reminder from Mr. Kingston's office that the next class should begin.

"Alexie, Lott. Andrew, Simon. Angaiak, Rachel," the teacher called out firmly. Mr. Townsend acknowledged each raised hand with a nod. He paused a moment, lifted his eyes, and surveyed the ninth-grade class. His eyes fell for a moment on Joseph, and Joseph felt an immediate surge of resentment rise within him. What are you looking at? Joseph challenged the teacher in his mind, but he held his voice in check.

Mr. Townsend looked quickly back toward his roll book, but before he could continue, two familiar figures in brown uniforms and trooper hats appeared in the opening that served as the classroom entrance. The class turned to look as Mr. Townsend stood.

"Excuse me," he said to the group. "Gentlemen." He

extended a hand beyond the entryway. Elena Nicholai went into high gear as soon as he was out of earshot, whispering loudly to everyone that they must be after the tire-slashing culprit.

The tiny class disintegrated into speculation and chatter as Joseph strained to hear the adult conversation. However, he could only see and not hear the three men. Trooper Rothman, the small one, seemed to be quietly explaining something to Mr. Townsend, using his hands once in awhile for emphasis.

Trooper Smith jumped in every so often, red-faced and firm. He pounded his fist against his open palm several times. Mr. Townsend stood back, arms folded across his chest, his blue eyes unreadable, saying nothing. Finally he shook his head, spoke a few words, and motioned toward his waiting students.

The troopers turned to leave, and Joseph let out the breath that he hadn't realized he was holding. Questions reeled in his head: Who were they asking about? What had they learned? Had they discovered footprints? And why were they talking with Mr. Townsend? Joseph pushed the questions aside, telling himself he didn't care, but still they nagged at him.

Mr. Townsend sat back at his desk as if nothing had happened, and the class quieted. "Benchley, Joseph," he read from the roll book. Joseph winced inside at the kass'aq name his father had left him, so out of place compared to the familiar names of the village. He raised his hand and lowered it, slowly and deliberately, challenging the teacher with his eyes, using a signal of disrespect that would probably go right by the white-haired stranger. No matter. He had other ways to make his point.

When roll call—all eleven names—was finished, Mr. Townsend gave each student a thin paperback volume. *I Heard the Owl Call My Name*, Joseph read from the cover.

"This is the story of a priest who finds himself, the only white man, thrust into a village in southeast Alaska and the challenges he must face," Mr. Townsend began.

"Yeah, they should have told him to go home," Joseph said. His voice was low but discernible. His classmates sat up and listened. Elena Nicholai raised her painted eyebrows and wound one finger nervously around a strand of hair.

"Some of them do," Mr. Townsend replied, taking a step toward Joseph, looking him squarely in the eye. "But he must decide—"

"I suppose he thought he would be the great white savior, bringing law and order to the savage natives," Joseph continued, his voice louder now.

"He must decide what it is within him—"

"Stupid rules of the church and stuff. Kass'aq poison!" Joseph folded his arms across his chest and locked eyes with the teacher, who now stood directly in front of him.

"—what it is within him that motivates him," Mr. Townsend continued. "As he pays attention to the human beings around him, he becomes a human being himself," the teacher concluded firmly.

"Humph! Never met a white man that acted like a human being." Joseph's voice had risen almost to a shout, a direct challenge. Mr. Townsend stared a moment at his challenger. Then he turned and walked back to the front of the classroom.

"Your task—for all of you—is to read this book and get to know this man, this human being. What are his struggles? His desires? His loves? How is he like you, though he's white? How is he different? Now," he finished firmly, "you may have the rest of class to begin to read."

The others opened their books and settled into their chairs, but Joseph wasn't about to give this rude man that satisfaction. He put his head down on the desk, atop his folded arms, closed his eyes, and waited to see what Mr. Townsend would do next.

But Mr. Townsend did nothing. Eventually the bell rang, and the students proceeded on the rotation from one of the three open classrooms to another, cycling through the three teachers and six subjects that would become their routine for the year.

Simon caught up with Joseph as the last bell of the day sounded, his backpack swinging as they bounded down the steps into the daylight. The sun was still shining, but it hung lower now in the sky, mocking them with the promise of all that a day outdoors might have been.

"You don't like that new teacher much, do you?" Simon asked.

"Should I?" Joseph replied, expressionless.

"Well, I don't know. He seems harmless enough."

"You never know," said Joseph, his face serious now. He really didn't know why his distrust ran so deep and came so quickly to the surface. "Maybe he's a serial killer, or a child molester, or—or—or maybe he's just a big jerk!" Joseph widened his eyes, exaggerating the serious look so that it was no longer serious.

"Yeah, just like you," Simon teased, grinning, and he took off running with Joseph at his heels. The village sped by as they ran, a blur of clothes hanging on lines in the sun, brightly painted houses, and children enjoying the fresh air after a long day inside.

That night at home, while the TV blared and cast its hue over the children huddled around it, Joseph took the slim paperback from English class out of his backpack. He thought about the teacher and his choice of reading materials. Did he want their pity, giving them a book about a poor white man alone in a native village? Well, he certainly wasn't going to get any pity from Joseph. That white man didn't belong, plain and simple. But Joseph started the first chapter. If he was going to keep up the argument, it would help to know the story. Besides, he liked to read. He got through the first three chapters before drifting off to sleep.

The next day, Elena Nicholai informed him that the troopers had left without a word being said about catching the vandal of their plane. Evidently they had made no inquiries into the illegal harvesting of fish, either—at least Joseph had heard nothing about it.

Joseph and his friends moved through the second day of classes much as they had on the first. The newness of beginning high school was already slipping from their lives. In English class, discussion of the book began.

"What kinds of cultural conflicts did Mark experience

in the village?" Mr. Townsend asked the class, leaning against the front of his desk with the slim, worn volume in his hand.

Elena Nicholai shot up her hand with fervor. "Customs," she said. "You know, burial and stuff like that." Her face was proud as the teacher nodded in agreement.

Simon, always attentive in class, scratched at his head and added to her reply. "It was more than just customs. It was a way of thinking about life."

Mr. Townsend nodded again. The discussion was going well. Joseph decided it was time to dive in. "Yeah, the native people think about life. The white man doesn't."

"I see," said Mr. Townsend. "Can you give us an example from the book?"

Ha! You think I haven't read it, but I have, Joseph thought. Aloud, he replied, "They think about how nature connects with man and how man must respect it."

"Yes," Mr. Townsend said, nodding slowly in agreement. He rose to a full standing position and used his copy of the book to point a challenge at the class. "Now, as you continue to read, see what Mark learns about the thoughtfulness and respect of his neighbors." Eyeing Joseph, he added, "And see if they learn anything from him."

Right, thought Joseph. Maybe they'll learn to drink and waste away in front of the TV and collect welfare checks the first of each month. Great learning.

As the rest of the class opened their books to read, Joseph's eyes wandered to the window, where the tundra and sky stretched out as far as he could see. A flock of sandhill cranes flapped their long wings in a rhythmic good-bye as they headed south after a summer of nesting among the uncountable lakes and sloughs of southwestern Alaska. Joseph recalled how all this water-drenched land looked from the air—as the cranes would see it, as he himself had seen it flying to town in the mail plane—like a saturated sponge, every pore brimming with water.

The departing birds signaled the start of fall hunting. Duck season was set to open Saturday, and as Joseph sat, confined within the four walls of this building, he longed for the freedom of traveling by boat, cutting through the early-morning air, watching the harmony of flight, and harvesting birds that his mother could pluck and store for the winter.

The sound of Mr. Townsend's voice broke his reverie. "For Monday, I want you to draft a short composition, a personality profile. Describe someone you know well."

Someone I know well, thought Joseph as he gathered his books. Faces rose up in his mind: Grandfather, his cousin Andrew Jacob, his mother, his brother, Sam. He knew them all well, so he had only to choose one. The assignment would be easy.

None of those subjects would add sufficiently to the skirmish he had begun with the new teacher, though. Joseph thought a moment more, and he had it—the topic that would make drafting this essay worthwhile. This new teacher laid snares for himself like a professional trapper. It was almost too easy.

FIVE

MY FATHER

My father's name is Michael Robert Benchley, and he's a jerk. In fact, he's the biggest jerk I know. He lives in Portland, Oregon. He moved there when I was eight years old. Once he wanted me to come visit him, but I wouldn't go there if you paid me.

My mother met him when he was here as a construction worker in the village, helping to build the power plant. She must have been too young and dumb or something, because she married him even though he's white. My grandfather had to show him everything—how to set a net, trap beavers, shoot a moose, even how to get to Bainbridge on a snow-go. So you see, my father isn't very smart.

My father had kind of longish hair and a beard, at least he did the last time I saw him, which was before he left. The only thing he ever got good at was carving. He used to carve all kinds of animals out of soapstone. Seals, caribou, moose, salmon, and bears. When I was six, he got me my own knife, and we used to sit on the steps and carve together.

He had a loud voice and a loud laugh, but he got really quiet just before he left. When he left, he was sneaky. There was just a note and some money on the table. My mom was sad for a long time, but not me. Who needs him? He sends us money sometimes still, but I think my mom should just send it back. We can get by just fine without it. He calls once in awhile, too, but only my sisters go to the phone. I never want to talk to him again.

Like I said, my dad's the biggest jerk I know.

JOSEPH PUT DOWN HIS PEN, folded the paper, and stuffed it in his book. There, that was done. Probably not what old Mr. Townsend expected, but that was good. Keep him guessing.

The weekend had arrived at last. The morning air hung still and quiet in the small house, and he could hear the rhythmic breathing of his sisters, his mother, and Sam in the other room. Maybe next year Sam would be old enough to go with him, Joseph thought as he sipped hot tea from a chipped mug. Out the window, he could see that the sky was finally beginning to lighten along the eastern horizon, from deep black to a velvet blue, heralding the start of day.

He had awakened in the middle of the night, unable to get back to sleep, brimming with the anticipation of this long-awaited Saturday and his first solo hunting trip. True, it was only for birds and he wouldn't be going far along the maze of sloughs and lakes, but

Grandfather had entrusted him with the boat, saying his bones ached too much in the early morning to get up for bird hunting.

Joseph hadn't even asked Simon to go with him, not wanting to spoil the adventure of going alone. He rose from the table, leaving the half-finished cup of tea cooling there, and pulled on his mud boots and rain jacket. He grabbed the shotgun and some shells and headed out, shutting the door gently behind him.

The wind blew the brisk morning air against his face, and the neighboring houses were shadowy shapes in the semidarkness. He was a man, getting up early to hunt food for the family, carrying on the tradition of his people. His eyes easily discerned their own boat, one among many along the shore, and he felt the pride of being the first one out.

Joseph set his gun, rain gear, and pack in the boat. Gently he pushed off and rowed for a while, using no motor to break the silence. His strength reached down the oars, pushing hard against the water—splash and push, splash and push. He was the force, the noise, the motion, repeated through his ancestors since the beginning of time.

Joseph was almost sorry when the moment came to pull the starter cord of the motor. He had paddled down the river and up the slough toward Igayik Lake, far enough from the village that the noise would disturb no one. Colors now streaked the eastern sky with orange and gold, welcoming him to the day. It would be a good day, a successful trip.

He had to tug hard on the rope, but the motor started

on the first pull. Joseph gunned the throttle twice and watched the blue exhaust dissipate into the semi-darkness. Then he put the motor in gear and maneuvered the boat along the glassy slough. He felt the power in his throttle hand, not as satisfying as the muscle strength he had used to propel the boat this far, but those muscles were weak now with exertion.

When he reached Igayik Lake, Joseph scanned the shoreline in the feeble daylight. He picked out a bay about a third of the way around the lake, where the grasses would make good cover.

Once at the bay, Joseph lifted an oar to check the depth. Finding it shallow, he maneuvered with the oars again, picking his way to a spot where the water grass stood tall on all sides. Perhaps he would have the lake to himself, Joseph thought. He felt the satisfaction of a man alone and in control of his world.

Only twenty minutes or so had passed before Joseph heard the first flock of sandhill cranes cackling in the distance. Their long necks and angled wings stretched forward in the sky, too far up for Joseph to get a good shot. He sat back and waited, enjoying the rich tones as they called to one another from high above him.

Joseph cupped his hands around his mouth and made a gutteral sound deep in his throat, mimicking the call of the cranes as his grandfather had taught him. But the cranes passed by. Before long, Joseph heard a big flock of Canada geese honking above. He tracked them with his eyes as they flew lower and lower, coming to rest not far from his boat. The sun had now lifted above the horizon, casting its light through a low gray layer of clouds. Joseph could see the birds as they spread out across the lake, bobbing for food, their white breasts flagging his attention.

He picked up his gun and rose slowly, taking careful aim above the camouflaging grasses. *Steady, slow, patient*—his grandfather's words reminded him as he focused his sights on a big bird some thirty yards away.

Suddenly the roar of a motor rose up in the distance. Another hunter was moving in on Joseph's carefully chosen spot. A shot rang from Joseph's gun, but it was too late. The geese, including his goose, the one he had in his sights, had already lifted their wings in flight. *Boom!* Joseph got off another shot at his bird in the air, and a feather flew. He pumped and fired once more, hitting a wing as the flock dispersed.

It was a strong bird, though, and it flew low and straight in a desperate attempt to rejoin the flock before it finally tumbled from the sky over the tundra a quarter mile from the lake. Joseph scowled and dropped his gun. Perhaps he could find the goose, but it would be a difficult search.

Joseph's anger with the unseen hunter mounted with his embarrassment over taking such hasty, wasteful shots. Perhaps, with the noise of the motor, the intruder hadn't heard the shots. If only he could get out of there before the other boat drew in too close. He looked again to fix in his mind the location where the bird had fallen, then he revved the motor to life.

But when he started forward, he felt the prop dig low in the mucky bottom. Joseph hit the kill button and yanked the motor up. Silt and weeds dripped from the prop. In his haste, he had forgotten to row out of the shallows.

As he sank crestfallen back to his seat, the roar of the motor that had caused the birds to fly became a deafening sound. Who would be so stupid? Joseph thought. At this rate, he'll come crashing through these weeds and smash my boat. Suddenly the motor died and he heard only the sound of the splashing wake, close enough that it rocked his boat.

Joseph peered through the weeds. There, at the helm of a tiny boat, stood Mr. Townsend in full rain gear, evidently surveying the shoreline for a good duck blind. Great, Joseph thought. First he ruins my shot, and now he'll probably take over my blind.

When Mr. Townsend sat and began to row, though, it was toward a patch of weeds just beyond the bay where Joseph sat. His first hunting trip alone, spoiled by this kass'aq. A soft rain began to fall. There was no sense staying in this spot. He must find that big goose, or it would go to waste.

So Joseph pushed his way out of the weeds with his oars. When the waters below darkened, signaling greater depths, he reached for the rope to start the motor.

"Joseph!" The new teacher's voice rang out from his patch of weeds. He was standing tall now, waving in Joseph's direction.

Joseph gave the rope a hard pull and gunned the motor. A loud roar and a cloud of blue smoke hung in the air as he pulled away without a wave or even another look in the direction of his teacher.

He careened across the lake, slowing down only when he reached a slough that meandered off across the tundra in the general direction where his bird had fallen. He wove around the bends of that slough and then another, trying to gauge the spot where the goose lay. Distance was so difficult to measure. How did Grandfather do it?

Joseph got out of the boat in three different spots, his boots sinking and sloshing along the wet ground as he walked in big circles, panning the ground for the black, white, and gray carcass.

Finally, with hunger gnawing at his stomach, he gave up the search. Full daylight was upon him now, a hazy, gray glare that hurt his eyes. He pointed the bow of the boat away from the scene of his early-morning disaster, the lake full of promise that had been destroyed by Mr. Townsend. He wished he were a shaman, with power to command the birds. Stay away from there, he would tell them. Don't let that white man shoot you.

Joseph found another good blind in the maze of lakes, but in the fullness of day he could hardly expect to shoot anything. He chewed on dry fish and pilot bread from his pack and stewed over his bad luck. Not luck, really, but interference of a white man who should stick to buying his food at the Bainbridge stores, not go shooting from the sky what belonged to Joseph's people.

As he sat in his boat, the light rain ceased and the wind picked up. The air, though cool, seemed stifling. Finally, Joseph decided to go in.

His anger mounted with every bump of the boat across the tiny waves. His first hunting trip alone ruined. What would he say to his family and friends when he returned empty-handed? No matter that none of the other fourteen-year-olds had gone out alone; most of them had fathers to hunt with. It was embarrassing.

He was still pondering the awkwardness of it all, and caressing his anger, when he turned onto Long River. The village loomed into view—the school, the fuel tanks towering by the river, the boat-dotted shoreline. Hopefully he wouldn't pull right up next to someone with a boat full of birds. Hopefully . . .

His hopes were for nothing. There was Elena Nicholai, strutting along the shore where the boats were tied. Joseph considered for a moment speeding up and continuing down the river just to avoid her, but feeling heavy fatigue in his body and mind, he turned in and cut the motor. She was already talking to him in her grating voice as the forward momentum pushed the boat toward shore.

"Joseph, good to see you. How's the hunting today? Did you get some ducks? A crane? A goose? Where's your grandfather? Joe Henry and his dad came in a little while ago with a whole boat full of geese—big Canadians. You should have seen! I bet they had at least ten, or maybe eight. It was a lot, anyway. Joe shot four of them himself. His dad was pretty proud."

She paused to catch her breath. She must be the most talkative Eskimo in the world, Joseph thought. The boat eased to shore with a thud. He jumped out and pushed the anchor into the dark, wet sand.

"So what about you, huh?" Elena was already at the edge of the boat, craning her neck to see Joseph's catch.

Joseph grabbed for his rain gear, gun, and pack. "Nothing," he mumbled under his breath.

"Nothing?" Elena screeched. "Why, Joseph Benchley, you're a better hunter than that. I've seen you come in with just dozens of birds when you've gone with your grandfather." She batted her eyes twice in his direction, but Joseph remained fixed on the path before them.

"I said nothing, OK?" he said harshly. It would be worse to tell her the whole story, how he had wasted a bird because of a stupid kass'aq. His people deplored waste of any kind. Elena would spread it all over the village. She was like a one-person telephone network.

Unless he could tell it so the blame fell where it really belonged. They were at his front steps now, Elena almost panting at his side. He turned and sat, dropping the gear in the tall grass. Elena immediately sat, too. She moved close to Joseph on the narrow step. He hoped no one walked by and saw them.

"Well, I did shoot one big Canadian goose, right as soon as I got out there, see." Joseph turned and looked her full in the face for effect. She wasn't quite so ghastly without all the school-day makeup.

"I got up really early and had this super blind in the grasses over on Igayik Lake," he said.

"That's a long way," Elena said with respect.

"Yes, but this was a great spot, and no one else was there. The sun was just coming up, and a huge flock came in. I waited until I could get my sights on a huge one swimming about thirty yards away." He could see Elena was taking this all in.

"And then?" she asked.

"And then who should come roaring across the lake but Mr. Townsend. And just as I'm about to shoot, he starts flock-shooting, see. Bang! Bang! Bang!" Joseph pounded his fist on the step to make his point, and Elena drew back.

"He must have shot ten times," Joseph continued, "and I'll bet he killed or injured four birds. They fell from the sky, all over the tundra in different spots. And then Townsend just turns and drives away, leaving those birds there to rot. He probably went off to another lake and wasted four more."

He paused to let his words sink in. Elena's eyes were huge. "No," she said. "He wouldn't just shoot them and leave them."

"What do you expect?" Joseph replied. "He's a kass'aq. They're all like that."

"But your fa—" Elena stopped short. No one ever talked to Joseph about his father. "But you wouldn't think he'd be so open about it. Didn't he see you?"

"No. Once he started blasting, I hid down in the weeds where he couldn't see. I told you it was a good blind. He never knew I was there."

"Oh, my," said Elena. "What about the geese? You went after them, didn't you?"

"That's why I never got any myself. I felt so bad about those geese that I spent all morning looking everywhere for them. But it was tough to keep track of where they fell, and some of them were so high when he shot that they could have landed anywhere. I didn't find a one." Joseph shook his head in disgust.

"Of course, what else could you do?" Elena spoke the words softly. She sounded sincere, compassionate, as she put her hand on Joseph's knee. He was surprised at how warm and right it felt there. "Are you going to turn him in?" she asked.

"I don't know. What do you think I should do?" Joseph looked deep into her eyes, and she turned away, blushing ever so slightly and withdrawing her hand.

"Well, he certainly should get in trouble for it. But it would be his word against yours," Elena said.

"Yeah, that's the problem," Joseph agreed. "There isn't any proof, not without those birds."

"Maybe we could go back out after them. I could help you look." Elena's face was eager, and Joseph smiled at her for the first time that he could remember. Then he shook his head.

"No, I couldn't ask you to do that for me. It would be a long search and probably useless. The foxes will be after those birds, if they haven't got them already." Joseph sighed, and disappointment hung on Elena's face.

"I'm tired, Elena." Joseph couldn't believe he was speaking so civilly to her. "I'm going in." He stood up, and she rose beside him. "Thanks for listening," he added. Before today, he hadn't thought she was capable of listening, and he felt a twinge of guilt that the story he'd confided had been untrue.

"No problem," she said in the same soft voice. With a smile, she headed down the boardwalk toward her house next door. Maybe she wasn't quite such a pest after all, Joseph thought as he watched her retreat. And her famous mouth was going to serve his purposes well.

Six

By the end of the second week of school, the story of Mr. Townsend's wanton waste of birds had circulated through practically the whole village, as near as Joseph could tell. As early as Monday, students had begun eyeing their teacher with suspicion, and at least three of Joseph's classmates related the tale back to him, pretty much as he had told it to Elena Nicholai, though she had evidently removed his name from it, for the story always began with "Someone saw . . ."

Joseph wasn't sure how to gauge the full power of this rippling undercurrent of untruth, nor was he sure what exactly to think of it. He had never made a habit of lying, but then he had never made a habit of slashing plane tires, either. Still, doing damage to government property felt more remote than doing damage to a teacher whom he had to face daily. Not that he liked Mr. Townsend, but he felt little satisfaction when everyone met the teacher with cold looks and hostile comments. Somehow it was different from when Joseph himself was harsh with the man; in those cases, Joseph always knew he was in control and could stop when he wanted.

But this rumor was far beyond his control. Joseph knew, too, how strong his people could be, how negative when they wanted to communicate their dislike, especially for an outsider. His mother, who seemed to think about these things, said it was part of how the Yup'ik people had survived for centuries in a harsh environment. Order had to be maintained, she said, and everyone had to be dependable.

Even Simon and his family had suffered when they first arrived in Napamiut, though they were Yup'ik, too, and had only come from a neighboring village. People had spread rumors about them stealing gas and drinking in private. Joseph found the rumors to be untrue when he got to know Simon and his family, but the lies lingered in the village for years, like a relentless current in a river.

Not that Joseph felt sorry for Mr. Townsend. He was an intruder, like all the kass'aqs, and, in particular, he had intruded on Joseph's hunting space. But still, Joseph wasn't a hundred percent sure he'd tell the story again, given the same opportunity. He really hadn't planned it; it had just slipped out.

Amazingly, he still felt a little bad about deceiving Elena Nicholai, too. She had been discreet in her dealings with Joseph all week, as if this secret had drawn them together in a respectful relationship. She kept a guarded distance in class, and though she would sometimes join up with him as he walked to or from school, she held back her usual chatter and prodded him to speak instead about the details of his daily life: the water that needed to be hauled; the times he read with his brother, Sam; the hours he sat with his grandfather. Her attention made Joseph feel special in an odd sort of way, more than her fawning and chattering ever had.

That she had changed in conjunction with his confiding of a lie made Joseph feel more than a little off-balance.

When Joseph took his seat in English class that Friday, he noticed the worn look that had been building on Mr. Townsend's face since Monday. His eyes, normally piercing and calm, looked tired; his mouth, usually firm, drooped at the corners in a half frown. Joseph was sure the rumors had reached his ears early in the week. And now, perhaps someone—Alexie John, for instance—had made the concerns of the villagers known, in a roundabout way, of course. Perhaps they had even asked him to leave. Good, Joseph tried to tell himself. One less kass'aq. But his heart felt sick at the degree of damage he might have done.

The class began with twenty minutes of quiet reading in books of their choice. But Joseph found himself staring at the words, not taking in a bit of it, but turning a page every once in awhile for effect.

"Let's move on," Mr. Townsend announced at last, breaking the silence. A ripple of chatter spread through the room as the students closed their books.

"I have a poem to share with you today," the teacher continued. Despite his haggard appearance, his voice rang firm and in control as always.

"The title is 'Do Not Go Gentle Into That Good Night,' written by the Welsh poet Dylan Thomas. In some ways it goes along with the theme of death that we've been discussing in *I Heard the Owl Call My Name*. I'd like for you to consider what it says on that theme and what other applications it might have."

When he finished introducing the poem, Mr. Townsend gave each student a xeroxed copy. Then he began to read in a hushed voice that built to a booming sound and died off with the rhythm of the words.

> Do not go gentle into that good night,
> Old age should burn and rave at close of day;
> Rage, rage against the dying of the light.

I'm not old, Joseph thought. But I've felt rage against the dying of our ways, the old ways, that Grandfather has spoken of. It is like the poet says, like a light that is fading, leaving us in darkness. He pondered the thought, surprised at the connection he felt with a poet from another country and time.

Mr. Townsend had continued reading, and Joseph had to find his place on the xeroxed sheet.

> Wild men who caught and sang the sun in flight,
> And learn, too late, they grieved it on its way,
> Do not go gentle into that good night.

How does a person catch the sun, Joseph wondered. Or sing it? Or more curious yet, grieve it on its way? The words made the sun seem a living creature, fully interacting with humans, in a way that might be part of Grandfather's stories. Surely this Welsh man was a kass'aq, but his thinking here seemed almost Yup'ik.

Mr. Townsend's voice pulled Joseph's thoughts back, and he realized the teacher was at the end of the poem.

> And you, my father, there on the sad height,
> Curse, bless me now with your fierce tears, I pray,
> Do not go gentle into that good night.
> Rage, rage against the dying of the light.

The power of this final stanza stunned Joseph. The poems he'd heard in grade school were little rhymes and ditties. This one sounded like the wind as it wrapped stinging snow around a house, and like the loon that cried alone in the night. He sat up, hoping Mr. Townsend would read the whole thing over, so he could catch the parts he'd missed.

But the teacher's own words followed. "There is much we could discuss about this poem, and I'm sure we'll only skim the surface today. Let's begin by hearing some words or phrases that especially caught your attention."

" 'Old age should burn and rave at close of day,' " offered Simon, his voice serious.

Mr. Townsend nodded. "Others?" he prompted.

" 'And you, my father, there on the sad height,' " added Rachel. Her tone was wistful.

"Yes—the powerful context for the poem—the impending loss of a father. Anyone else?" Mr. Townsend looked around.

" 'Rage, rage against the dying of the light,' " Joseph surprised himself by speaking the words of the poet in a voice that mirrored Mr. Townsend's.

"I had picked that line, too," Mr. Townsend said, leaning back against the edge of his desk, his feet crossed at the ankles. "What does it say to you, Joseph?"

"I—I'm not sure. I like the sound of it—forceful, and important." He struggled for the words and suddenly wished he had kept quiet.

"That it is," agreed Mr. Townsend. "It speaks of asserting yourself against an enemy, death. It's a losing battle, of course, but Dylan Thomas wants us to fight it just the same." He paused a moment, glanced down at his feet, and began to speak again, louder now.

"Perhaps I chose to share this poem with you for that very reason. Sometimes we don't feel we have the strength or energy to fight the battles we never asked for, against forces we don't even understand. But the poet tells us to rage."

"Isn't too much rage a bad thing?" asked Simon, his eyes puzzled behind his glasses.

The teacher stood up straight. "Certainly it is. It can destroy us and others around us. But doing nothing—that can be a problem, too."

The teacher cleared his throat and, after a moment of silence, continued. "I've been struggling with that very question myself this week. I've felt rage, but I haven't known what to do about it." All the students sat up now, listening.

"I suppose that most, if not all, of you have heard by now the rumor that's been going around about me—that I shot several birds wantonly and left them to die on the tundra. I want to say to all of you right now"—he paused a moment to make eye contact with each of the eleven students—"that this rumor is totally false."

Joseph swallowed hard. He wondered what Elena was thinking. This kind of confrontation was the last thing he had expected. In the village, rumors were swallowed like bitter pills. People had to stick together, and that took precedence over sticking up for yourself, as Mr. Townsend was doing. Still, it was a gutsy thing to do.

"So I want to rage, but I don't know against whom or what," Mr. Townsend said. "Perhaps just against the injustice, and the untruth, of it all. But you all know that I am in a precarious position here. I am the intruder, the outsider." His eyes fell on Joseph. "The hated one, for some. Who would believe me?

"Nevertheless, I feel I must speak. The dying light for me, in this circumstance, is the dying of truth rather than of life, though sometimes the two are difficult to distinguish. How can we live if we live a lie? So I must rage, even if quietly, against this untruth. I must come boldly before you and declare my innocence."

The room was still as a winter night. No one made the slightest movement.

"Well, then, I've said my piece, and taken too much of your class time to do it," Mr. Townsend concluded, leaning back against the desk again. The tension in the room unlocked with rustling and shuffling.

"Now we'll have to finish our discussion of Dylan Thomas another day," the teacher said. Already the students were folding their papers into their books, glad to have the heavy veil of honesty lifted. Joseph, however, still felt a heaviness that hung about him like a rope. He stared at the top of his desk, hoping for the bell to ring.

"Oh—your compositions, the personality profiles you handed in on Monday—I have them here for you to pick up." Mr. Townsend's voice was normal, businesslike again. He spread the set of papers across his desk. "Please retrieve your papers and prepare a second draft for next Monday, paying attention to my comments in red."

The bell sounded, and the students gathered about the desk to get their work. Joseph searched quickly and grabbed his, anxious to leave the room. But a large SEE ME was penned across the bottom of his short essay. He looked up to see if Mr. Townsend would notice if he quietly left, but it was too late. The teacher was staring right at him.

"Joseph," he said quietly, and nodded toward the chair beside his desk. As the other students filed out, murmuring to one another about their teacher's remarks, Mr. Townsend pulled out his padded chair and sat down, his hands folded on the desktop in front of him. Joseph sat and stared at the floor, suddenly terrified of all the subjects that Mr. Townsend could potentially broach.

"First of all," he began, "your composition. I didn't write any comments on it, because I want you to know that I respect the powerful feelings it conveys. However, it does need work. Your reader needs to be able to experience more of the man that your father is and was, not just your reactions to him. How does he look when he laughs? When he's angry? How does his voice sound? What specific activities do you remember doing with him?"

The teacher paused to let the suggestions sink in, but Joseph's inner voice was reeling in response. Remember him—the way he looked, sounded, acted? Why would I want to? I did what you asked the first time, and now you want to dig some more in my memories. Joseph knew at that instant that this assignment of rewriting was one he would never complete.

Without looking up, Joseph folded the paper and rose to leave.

"Not so fast," Mr. Townsend said. Eyes still on the floor, Joseph sat back down. "There's a greater issue we need to discuss today."

He knows, Joseph thought. He knows I started the rumor. That rage he was talking about is saved for me. Joseph struggled for what he would say in response, but no defense came to mind.

"I'm sure you recall," Mr. Townsend began, "that there was a little incident here just before the start of school. The tires of a Fish and Game plane were slashed—a substantial amount of damage done, not to mention inconvenience."

The tires, Joseph thought. He had all but forgotten. What did Mr. Townsend have to do with them? The rumor should be this man's concern now.

The teacher continued. "It happens that I was on the tundra near the airstrip when the—uh—incident occurred, though I don't think the, um, perpetrator saw me."

Joseph swallowed hard. His teacher knew all about his misdeed. How unlucky could he be? Had Townsend already reported him to the authorities?

He could feel Mr. Townsend's penetrating gaze, and he dared not look up. The teacher cleared his throat and continued. "I informed the troopers that I had seen the incident and could identify their suspect, a school-age male, upon meeting with the students on the first day of school. And, in fact, I was able to identify him."

Joseph felt his face grow hot even as he stared intently at the floor. Mr Townsend continued, "However, I chose not to reveal the identity of this person to the troopers.

Instead, I gave my word that I would speak with the young man within ten days and then report back to them."

And then what, Joseph wondered. Visions of the juvenile detention center in Bainbridge flashed through his mind.

"The ten days are nearly up," Mr. Townsend continued, tapping his pencil on the desk. "And I've worked out this plan. You make payments of fifty dollars twice a month—say the first and third Mondays—during the school year. I'll send the money to the troopers. By the end of the year, the damages will be paid off, with interest, and the case will be closed. Your identity will be withheld and the authorities will not become involved, as long as you make your payments regularly, through me, to the troopers."

He paused for Joseph's reaction.

Joseph looked up. "The troopers will agree to this?" he asked softly. He remembered Trooper Smith's angry face at the meeting.

"Yes," Mr. Townsend answered. "I proposed the concept to them before they left, and they went along with it. Given the tension about the closed fishing season, they were happy enough to forgo an investigation. They just want to be compensated for the damages. So—you agree to make the payments?" His tone was direct.

"Yes," Joseph replied. What choice did he have? He was getting off easy, all things considered, especially since he'd been so harsh with Mr. Townsend right from the start. At least it seemed his teacher didn't know the truth about the rumor—or he would hardly be so generous. Joseph drew in a breath and waited, trying not to look panicked.

"Well, I guess that's it," Mr. Townsend concluded, offering a half smile and extending his hand. Joseph gripped and shook on the deal, but he didn't smile. He had been taken captive by the enemy. And where would he get that kind of money?

Seven

Simon leaned against the step railing and waited for his friend. A cool wind had blown away the low gray clouds that had hung in the air that morning, clearing a bright blue sky above the tundra, now a patchwork of rusty autumn browns and reds. The slender, pointed leaves of the scrub willows, as close to a tree as one could see here, had turned a fiery orange. In just a few weeks, the wind would blow in snow with the clouds. Autumn was barely long enough to call a season.

Joseph burst through the double doors. "I was beginning to think you'd left early or something," Simon remarked, swinging his pack to his shoulder.

"Yeah, I should have," Joseph growled.

"Why? What happened?"

"Oh, nothing," Joseph said. He was in too deep now to confide even in his best friend. Besides, he didn't want anyone thinking that Townsend had cut him any favors. "Hey, what about that Townsend?" he added, forcing a lighter tone into his voice. Simon was thoughtful; he would be a good gauge of the class's reaction to the teacher's revelations.

"That was wild," Simon observed. "Pretty smart of him, really, to defend himself in public. I mean, what did he have to lose? People were saying the worst about him anyway."

"Yeah, but—he was so direct. Maybe he's just a great liar," Joseph said.

"Maybe," Simon nodded. "It kind of makes you think, though, about rumors and all. Like, why do people love to gossip and make somebody else look bad?"

Joseph said nothing, so Simon continued. "Remember when we first came here, back when I was in fourth grade? People started saying my dad was an alcoholic. No one ever said it to his face, but kids would make jokes to me about whiskey bottles and beer. I wouldn't say anything, but I'd cry when I got home." He paused and swallowed. Joseph wondered if it still hurt after all these years.

"It was so unfair," Simon went on. "My dad never went near liquor his whole life, at least not that I know of. Here he was, a pastor, trying to set a good example. And people lied about him. I remember once I screamed at him to do something about it, to make them stop. But he just put his arm around me and said we needed to be patient. When people got to know us, he said, they would slowly put the rumor to rest."

"Maybe he should have said something from the pulpit—you know, kind of like Townsend did in class today," Joseph said.

"Maybe. But I can't imagine a Yup'ik doing that."

Joseph nodded. "Could work for a kass'aq, though." He slowed the pace of their walk and turned to his friend. "Did you ever find out who started the rumor about your dad?"

"Never did," Simon replied. "I have some suspicions, though. Elena Nicholai's mom, for one. She loves to gossip, and she always used to give my mom dirty looks—still does, sometimes."

"Your mom?" Joseph asked. Simon's mom was soft-spoken and polite, a lot like Joseph's mom. She was a hard worker, too, putting up lots of fish in the summer and knitting socks and mittens all winter long for the Ladies' Aid Society at the church.

"Yeah. When I thought about it later, I wondered if maybe she was jealous or something, since my mom tries so hard to set a good example."

"Maybe," Joseph agreed. They were passing right by the Nicholai's house at that moment, and they both turned their heads. There was Elena's mom, hanging out clothes with her cousin Hannah. Hannah, who was best friends with Joseph's mom, was thankfully not much like her older cousin. Even from the boardwalk, they could see Gertrude Nicholai's chin waggling in what could only be animated gossip. Simon looked at Joseph and shrugged with a smile. Joseph smiled back, and his earlier bad temper seemed mostly just a memory.

Joseph turned his head once more to see if Elena was there with the older women, a gossip-in-training among the fluttering sheets and underwear. He saw no sign of her. Perhaps she was at her dad's store, where she sometimes stocked shelves or swept after school. He smiled slightly to think that he cared what Elena was up to. On school days she wore that awful makeup and sprayed her hair stiff. Still, there was a different part of her he was coming to see—more human and compassionate. The cackle of her mother's laugh rang in his ears. He could see how the brash and talkative side of Elena had come to be.

The boys entered Joseph's house together, and Joseph flung his pack on the bed where the three younger children were in their usual spots in front of the blaring TV.

"Hi, Simon," Dora called out, putting on her best smile. Simon nodded in her direction, and Joseph shook his head. It was hard to believe that his sister liked to smile at boys now; for most of her twelve years, she had made every effort to get away from them.

Joseph rummaged through the kitchen cupboard and pulled out a large can of whole chicken. From the refrigerator he took two carrots and an onion.

"Grandfather has rice, I think," he said to Simon, handing him the vegetables. "I want to go over and make him some soup. His bones have been aching more lately, and he hasn't wanted to come by for supper. Come with me?"

"Sure," Simon agreed. He fell in behind Joseph as he charged back out the door.

They found Joseph's grandfather sitting at the kitchen table, putting the finishing touches on a bearded seal he had been carving from soapstone. Joseph hadn't carved for many years. His fingers longed to touch the smooth gray stone and feel it transformed through the power of his knife.

But he and Simon set instead to the immediate task of feeding Grandfather. "You take good care of me, boys," the old man said. Joseph felt pride well up inside him. Grandfather had taken care of him and the rest of his family after his dad had left. It felt good to be able to help him now.

Joseph dumped the chicken, broth and all, into a large pot. Simon threw in crudely chopped carrots and onions, along with a handful of rice. A generous shake of salt and pepper completed the seasoning, and Joseph dipped a pitcher of water from the plastic barrel in the corner to thin the broth. He turned up the burner of the oil stove ever so slightly, and soon the steamy smell of chicken filled the room.

The boys sat, Joseph at the table and Simon on the bed, and watched as Frank Paul carved. Late afternoon sun slanted through the single window, casting a warm glow on their faces. No one spoke for a long time.

"Alqallaq." Simon broke the silence with the Eskimo name of Joseph's grandfather. "You're so quiet."

"Iii," the old man nodded slowly, setting down his knife. "We learn by silence, from the time that we are very small. If I want to teach you to carve, for instance"—he picked up the black-gray soapstone seal, stroking it lightly and then holding it cupped in his hand for them to see—"I pick up my knife and just begin. You watch. Then you take the knife and try. If you make mistakes, I show you the right way. This way you train your eyes and your mind. Today, children ask too many questions. They distract themselves, and they don't learn."

Simon nodded. "Some adults talk too much, also. You know—gossip."

"Iii," Grandfather agreed. "This is not a good thing.

But consider the old days. We had to work together as a group or none would survive in this harsh land. Each person had to be kept accountable by community opinion. Just like this animal here." He turned the seal in his hand, examining it closely.

"The eyes, the ears, the nose, the fins, the tail—each part of it is crucial to the animal's survival. Bad eyes, bad ears, bad nose—any of these, and the seal will die. So it is with people. No bad parts can stay."

"But why not just tell them if they're wrong, so they can change?" Simon asked.

"They must learn to sense and feel and listen with their whole being. Then they must discover for themselves, with this whole being, what is their mistake. And then they must correct it themselves. If they can't do this, they are a useless part of our community."

Grandfather's words pierced through the confusion in Joseph's head, crowded with thoughts of school and the kass'aq teacher. Mr. Townsend was the one at fault, after all, disturbing the order of things with his declaration of innocence. "The kass'aqs don't know this," Joseph said. "They are always loud and direct."

"Iii, their ways are different, but their world is different also. And their world is partly our world now, so who knows what to do?" Grandfather shook his head and set down the soapstone seal.

Joseph shuffled uneasily in his chair. A change of subjects was in order. "Tell us about how it was before the white men came," Joseph said. His eyes fell on the carved seal. "Tell how you went seal hunting on the coast as a young boy." He had heard before, but always his grandfather added some new detail.

Grandfather cleared his throat, his Adam's apple traveling up and down his leathery neck. "I was younger than you boys, probably nine or ten. We never used to know our age, until the white men came and would tell us just by looking at us. People weren't traveling with dogsleds in those days, so we would wake up before sunrise and just start walking.

"I was the only child in my family. Though there had been four others born to my parents, they all had died. We were at our winter camp in Angaicuak, on a big lake near the coastal area they now call Nelson Island. Remember that in those days people moved all the time, following the seasons and the wild game. We stayed in skin tents or sod houses and didn't really have permanent homes."

The boys nodded. What a carefree life, Joseph thought. He wished he had lived then instead of now—no school, no teachers, no kass'aqs, no planes, no money, no worries. He would have been at one with the land and the people, like the magnificent caribou, with their rich white manes and heavy antlers, that knew the vastness of the tundra from the Kilbuck Mountains to the Bering Sea. Grandfather's voice interrupted Joseph's reverie.

"On my first hunt, I walked for three full days, all day long, with my father, toward the west, where the sea ice was beginning to break. We stopped to camp only when it grew dark, sleeping on the ground without tents. We were fortunate to have good weather for our journey, for sometimes hunters would get caught in a spring blizzard or in days of fog. If they weren't careful, they could end up wandering in circles, never finding their way back to their people.

"When we reached the ice, we walked out onto it, looking for holes where the seals would come up for air. The soles of our mukluks were soft and pliable, and our feet were cushioned by the dry grass we stuffed inside the mukluks each autumn, so we could walk without a sound, better even than in those fancy sneakers you boys like to wear."

Joseph and Simon looked down at their feet and smiled. "Can't play basketball in mukluks, Grandfather," Joseph said. His grandfather smiled, showing a few gaps behind his bottom lip where teeth once had been.

"Anyway, we found a hole where the ice was thin, and my father motioned for me to lie down on my stomach as he did. Then we scooted ourselves slowly over to the edge of the hole."

"Weren't you afraid the ice would break and you would fall in?" Joseph asked. Every time he had heard the story, this moment stuck out as the most dramatic. Despite the abundance of water in the Kuskokwim Delta, none of the Yup'ik people he knew could swim.

"When you spread yourself out like that, the weight of your body is distributed," Grandfather explained. "And you listen carefully for cracking and shifting. I remember it being so quiet that all I could hear was my own breathing. I tried to make it as shallow as I could, so I would not scare off the seals.

"We lay there for a long time—maybe an hour or so.

You might think we would get very cold there on the ice, but actually we stayed quite warm, because we used all fur for winter clothes then.

"Suddenly the nose of a seal poked up through the hole, and my father's grip on his harpoon tightened. He rose up on all fours and plunged the harpoon below the surface, deep into the seal's flesh. The water in the hole turned bloodred, and he pulled the seal out with a grunt. It was a bearded seal, just like this one I have carved today." Grandfather paused and fingered the seal lightly.

"We hauled the seal back to the winter camp on a sled we pulled behind us. We met two small groups of hunters on the way and cut off a small piece of flesh for each of them, for luck.

"When we reached the camp, my mother came out with a serving spoon, which she filled with snow and shoved into the seal's mouth. She did this so the seal's spirit would not be thirsty and could return to the sea. Then she cut up the meat and boiled it like soup.

"While it cooked, she gathered a bowl from each of the tents in our camp. After filling them, she returned them one by one to their owners, and the people were satisfied."

He paused, and a twinkle came to his eyes. "That was when your grandmother first noticed me. She was only seven or eight at the time, but her mother pointed to me and proclaimed what a good hunter I was, providing seal meat for all the people. In those days, a girl was to look for a skilled, strong hunter to be her husband, and her family would arrange the marriage."

"So you didn't choose the one you would marry." Joseph had heard this before, but the notion still seemed strange. It would have saved his mother some heartache, though.

"For most people, this way was fine," Grandfather continued. "There weren't real marriages then, anyway, not before the churches were established. People stayed together, but if things didn't work out, they would go their separate ways."

What about the children? Joseph voiced the question only to himself.

Joseph rose and ladled three bowls of thick chicken soup from the pot. The steam warmed his face as he set one before his grandfather, handed one to Simon, and set the third at his own place at the table.

Joseph picked up his spoon. Grandfather coughed and said, "Let us pray." The boys dropped their heads as the old man spoke. "Thank you, Lord, for the food you have provided for us, and for these young men who know how to listen. Amen."

How his grandfather had shifted from a boyhood of animal spirits to these simple, pious prayers of the white man's God was beyond Joseph. It was another question he longed to ask, but he swallowed it instead, along with his soup. Asking too many questions would be impolite.

They ate in silence except for the slurping of the soup. When they finished, only the bones, licked clean of their meat, remained in the bottoms of their bowls.

"Good soup," Grandfather said. He wiped his chin with his sleeve.

"Not so good as that seal soup in the old days, I bet," Joseph said.

"Don't be fooled by your imagination, my grandson. Our life was good, but it was also hard. Times of starvation would come upon us, when the fish wouldn't run and the moose could not be found. Then we would grow thin on soups made by boiling our skin clothing, tents, and even kayaks. Mothers would give their young children mukluks to gnaw on when they cried from hunger."

"These years of hunger—they were before the white men and their hunting restrictions?" Joseph asked.

"Yes," Grandfather replied. "I know that now they speak of high-seas netting and commercial fishing that get in the way of our harvest, but there are fish at all times now. It wasn't always like that. Nature goes in cycles, but we haven't suffered starvation for many years."

"But who knows?" said Joseph defensively. "Some say the starvation will come again someday."

"Iii. Perhaps." Grandfather nodded.

"There's always canned chicken," Simon said with a grin, and he rose to set his bowl by the dishpan. "I need to get home. Mom will have another meal waiting for me. Joseph, I'm going to the community center tonight, if you want to shoot some pool."

Joseph nodded in agreement and gathered the other bowls. While his grandfather watched, he emptied out the bones, added hot water from the kettle to the standing dishwater, and cleaned out the bowls. He thought about talking with his grandfather concerning the disgust he felt for the kass'aqs, which was like a huge snag that caught up all of his thoughts. Talking about it might help him cast off the nagging guilt he felt over the plane and the teacher. But the last thing he wanted was to be a disappointment to his grandfather, and so he said nothing.

EIGHT

THAT NIGHT AT THE COMMUNITY CENTER, the worn green felt of the pool table and the smooth glide of the cue in Joseph's hand gave him a brief diversion from his dilemma. As he and Simon played through three games, only the back of his mind was troubled. There was comfort in the gathering of voices at the center: young men out of school, restless from a day of inactivity; high school girls, casual and chatting in T-shirts and jeans; and the young Village Public Safety Officer, silently overseeing the action in his official uniform. A shifting energy mingled with the stale cigarette smoke.

The older people of the village were in their homes, clearing the supper dishes, tending to their children, lighting the steam baths where the husband and wife could slip off later to wash and relax. At some steam baths only the men gathered, to contest their ability to endure the scorching heat and steam. The old men joined in, outlasting them all, with their thick skin and the tolerance of advancing years.

Long ago, all of the men, old and young alike, would have gathered nightly in the large community *qasgiq*, a steam house where elders would tell stories and occasionally a shaman would perform some feat of magic or healing. But the *qasgiq* tradition had died out long before Joseph was born, and he could only imagine it from his grandfather's description. The community center seemed like a feeble substitute, he thought.

"I've had enough," Joseph said after his friend sank the last ball of their third game. He reached to hang up the pool cue.

"Afraid I'll beat you again?" Simon asked with a grin.

Joseph shrugged his shoulders. From the corner of the room, Henry Alexie stepped forward.

"I'm not afraid you'll beat me," Henry said to Simon. His face was expressionless, and he did not acknowledge Joseph at all but spoke directly to Simon.

Joseph felt a wave of disgust come over him. Henry was his second cousin, five years older than him. Despite their blood relationship, Henry and Joseph had never been friends. Ever since their grade school days, Henry had been surly with his cousin, treating him as less than a real person, even though they were, of course, both Yup'ik—Real People.

Simon faced Henry without any sign of intimidation. "I think I'm done for the night," he said quietly, and he hung his cue beside Joseph's. Together, the friends stepped outside.

"What's his problem?" Simon asked, as much to the night wind as to Joseph.

Joseph shrugged at the star-studded sky. It was a question without an answer; explanations really didn't matter.

Simon hopped on his four-wheeler and waved a quick good-bye. Joseph watched as he careened down the single village trail into the darkness.

Joseph lingered a moment on the wooden steps of the

center. The wind, blowing its whispers through the tall grasses, had cleared the night sky, and the myriad of stars shown clear against the blackened canopy. There was the North Star, at the end of the Little Dipper's handle. It was a sure and steady light, always there when the clouds of night parted to reveal the way a man should go.

Joseph sighed. If only there were a clear beacon to show his way through the confusion that had been growing in his life like wild grasses in the spring sunshine. It had started simply enough—he had only wanted to carry on the traditions of his people, gathering fish from the river's ample supply to keep his family strong and satisfied during the long winter.

Then had come the mounting frustration and anger, driving him to an impulsive act of destruction. Joseph wanted to push the memory of it all from his mind, yet at the same time he wanted to examine it, to turn it over in his head and perhaps discover a pocket of escape, like a shaman who could fly through a tiny opening into the spirit world beyond.

Joseph thrust his hands in his pockets and began a slow walk toward home. The village was quiet, bedding down for the night. A few lights shone from tiny windows. The hum of the power plant generators and the frosty nip of air from the cusp of winter settled into his senses. Beyond the village lay uncharted darkness.

Footsteps behind him on the boardwalk, lighter and quicker than his own, broke the mood.

"Joseph?" It was Elena's voice. He could see only her profile in silhouette as she came alongside him. Public lights in the village were scarce—one at the community center, one on the school, one set back at his end of the village behind the co-op store.

"Hi, Elena." His voice sounded soft and caring, like when he spoke with his grandfather. Then he remembered the other prong of the dilemma that rose up before him: the lie he had told to Elena and the rebuttal Mr. Townsend had proclaimed to the class. What could he say now? He felt a sinking feeling, like boots in a mucky river bottom.

Elena, true to form, began the conversation. "What do you make of Mr. Townsend's speech today?" she asked. It was the very question he had been hoping she would not ask.

Joseph stopped and turned toward the river. He could hear the waves lapping against the shore. Elena stopped beside him. "I don't know," he answered.

"But I thought you said . . ." Elena started. Her words drifted into the wind, without conclusion. A moment of silence followed, then she started again. "He sounded sincere," she said.

"So you believe his story?" Joseph felt the anger rise in his throat like a white-capped wave, and his voice rang in the night. He felt an awkward, unbalanced sense of injustice. He turned and continued down the boardwalk.

Elena kept up the pace beside him. He felt her hand come up lightly to touch his arm and then fall back to her side.

"I didn't mean it like that," she said. "But you haven't been honest with me." Her voice caught on the words.

"Aw, Elena," was all he could say. They stood now at

the junction where the narrow boardwalk led off toward her house. "Come on. I'll walk you up."

They went up the short walkway without a word. Her house, much larger than his next door, loomed in darkness. Colored images danced from the television to the tune of canned laughter deep inside. They stopped at the steps. Joseph sat. His head hung down, and he reached back with both hands, stretching the tension in his neck. Elena sat beside him.

"So what's going on, Joseph?" Her voice was gentle, not a harsh demand.

After a moment he answered. "Sometimes I'm not even sure myself. It started with the fishing regulations, and those Fish and Game guys. You weren't there. You didn't see how the one man yelled at us, like children. I get so tired of the kass'aqs. Why can't they leave us alone?"

Elena nodded, and Joseph was encouraged to go on.

"Our land, our fish, our birds," he continued. "Our people respect these, using only what we need. We never claimed them for our own, never tried to push the white man out." He felt better as he spoke of the problem with these more general words.

"The white men think totally differently. Everything belongs to a region, a district, to be regulated in some way." He recalled the teacher barging through Igayik Lake with his noisy boat.

Joseph's voice grew louder, overtaking the TV voices from inside. "Now they have control, telling us what we can and cannot do, with no respect for our ways and our needs," he concluded.

"But what about you, Joseph? All of what you say is true, but it bothers you so much." Joseph heard her struggle for the words. "How could you— I mean what have you . . ."

"Elena, listen." Joseph turned toward her, suddenly inspired. "I need some money. Do you think— Is there any way—you could ask your dad, see if he needs any extra help at the store for the winter?"

Elena's half-formed questions slipped by unanswered. "Of course," she replied, and a smile lit her face in the darkness. "I'll speak to him about it tomorrow."

At that, Elena rose from the steps. "I'd better get in now. It's getting cold out here."

She was right. The cold wind stung their cheeks and ears, whistling around the corners of the scattered homes.

Joseph rose, too. "Thanks, Elena," he said. He wished he could see her better in the darkness. He thought of reaching for her hand, but instead he just added, "I really mean it."

As he turned down the boardwalk into the night, he wondered who was changing, him or Elena. She was no longer just an annoying voice. She was almost a friend.

NINE

It was the following Tuesday, just after math class, when Elena finally approached Joseph with an answer to his request. He had spent the intervening days trying not to think about his need to raise money, finding his stomach in knots whenever he did puzzle over it.

Elena's smile lifted Joseph's spirits before she even spoke. "I talked to my dad," Elena said. "You're to come in after school today. He thinks he can use you for stocking shelves and cleaning."

"Thanks, Elena," Joseph said.

"I'll walk over with you if you want," Elena added.

"Sure," said Joseph. Not that he would need her for introductions or anything. Her family had known his family for generations back, like everyone else in the village. Elena's father could be intimidating, though. He was a sharp businessman who had built up his little store into a thriving business. Elena was his oldest daughter, and Joseph knew how he doted on her. It would be nice to have her there when they discussed the potential job.

So far Mr. Townsend hadn't pushed the money issue with Joseph, but only a few days had passed since their first discussion of it. In fact, he seemed to be giving

Joseph little attention at all, and for his part, Joseph chose to act sullen but obedient. He dutifully wrote out assignments—with the exception of the rewrite on his father—did the reading, and kept his mouth shut. No one had yet commented on his new cooperative attitude.

When the bell rang at three o'clock, Joseph was just finishing a difficult weld on a sled runner in the school shop. Holding the edges just so and bringing in the flame was a challenge, and he found himself wishing he had more than two hands, or at least that he could take off the thick welding gloves. But his mounting frustration was squelched by delight at the power he yielded through the welding torch, using it to melt and mold metal.

The weld was complete. Joseph pulled off the hot helmet and bulky gloves to examine the results. Simon came up and looked over his shoulder.

"Not bad," he said, scrutinizing the cooling line of solder.

"Like you could do better." Joseph threw him a grin as he hung up the torch and shelved the gear.

"Maybe. I know I could do better than you at Horse. Let's stop at the basketball court on the way home," Simon suggested.

"I can't," Joseph said. "I'm starting a job today. Or I think I am, anyhow."

"Really?" said Simon. "Where?"

"At Nicholai's store," Joseph answered. He reached for his jacket and pack from the coatrack in the entryway.

"Nicholai's!" Simon exclaimed. "You'll have to put

95

up with Elena the Mouth. And her dad—he's kind of scary. Remember when he caught Sam stealing that pack of bubble gum?"

Joseph nodded. Sam had been only four, and Dora hadn't been minding him like she was supposed to. Mr. Nicholai had caught him right in the act, slipping a pack of gum into his coat pocket. Joseph hadn't been with them, but when he heard about the yelling Mr. Nicholai had done, he wished he had been there to yell right back. Now, he realized, it was a good thing he hadn't had the chance. He wouldn't have dared ask for a job if he'd made a scene like he'd wanted to.

"I think I can handle Mr. Nicholai. You know, do what he says, stay out of the way," Joseph said. "And Elena's not that bad in small doses."

"Well, better you than me," Simon added. "But why do you want a job anyway? Basketball starts in a few weeks, and wrestling after that."

Don't remind me, Joseph thought to himself. Not to mention winter trapping, which would begin in early November, too late to yield money for the payments he needed to make. Hardly anyone in the village worked, adult or teenager. Only a handful of jobs were available, spread among the school, the village offices, and the store.

Aloud, Joseph said, "Well, I need the money."

"Don't we all?" Simon agreed. Still, he looked puzzled. "But what do you need it for?"

Responses raced through Joseph's mind, from "none of your business" all the way to the stark truth. But he didn't want to be rude, and the brute honesty of the mess he'd gotten into was too much to reveal even to his best friend. For some reason, an image of his mother, bearing a look of crushed disappointment as she surely would if she knew about the tire slashing, flashed before him. The image inspired an answer.

"My mom," Joseph said. "You know how she does skin sewing for extra money." He pictured her, bent over a pair of mukluk soles, tugging at the razor-sharp needle threaded with floss. "I thought I could make enough money by Christmas to get her one of those heavy-duty sewing machines at Bainbridge Commercial Company."

As he spoke the words, his heart lightened at the satisfaction of the clever answer, thought of so quickly. Then it sank like a diving bird, weighed down with guilt. His mother really could use a machine like that, and it was his place now, growing into the man of the household, to help her get it. But with the airplane debt— Well, maybe he'd make enough to pay for both. It was a wisp of hope, but he wrapped it tightly in his thoughts.

At the doorway of the school, Simon hollered at his second cousin, who was already hurrying down the steps. "Frank! Wait up! You want to shoot some baskets?" Frank halted and Simon took off, looking back for just a second at his friend. "Don't work too hard," he said with a grin.

Joseph sighed. The price had to be paid, but he didn't have to like it, any more than he liked the kass'aqs in the first place.

"Hi, Joseph." Elena stepped up beside him. "Ready to go?"

Joseph nodded and they went down the boardwalk in silence. The clouds had settled back in, forming a hazy gray canopy above. Joseph had flown once to Anchorage in a jet from Bainbridge, and as the plane climbed, it had broken through a cloud cover just like this into brilliant sunshine and blue sky. The clouds had made a puffy floor below the jet, in total contrast to the gray ceiling he had seen from the ground. Joseph was used to the gray, but he wished he could rise above to the light as easily as that jet had.

"Joseph, you know my dad," Elena started in. Joseph hoped she wouldn't get long-winded. "He can be kind of rough, but he really is sweet underneath. I mean, you just have to get to know him."

I don't need to get to know him, Joseph thought. I never got to know my own dad, and that hasn't hurt me any. I just need the job. Aloud, he said nothing, and Elena continued.

"He worked hard to build up that store. He always tells me how he planned it way back when he was in school, that he could own a store and make good money. He concentrated on his schoolwork—math and whatnot. He says you have to learn to think kass'aq if you want to succeed in business."

"Think kass'aq? Why?" Nothing sounded more foolish, or distasteful, to Joseph.

"Oh, I don't know. I guess they do things differently—profit and loss, competition—that sort of thing. And he's always having to deal with businesses in Bainbridge, in Anchorage, in Seattle even. I hear him on the phone, arguing over prices and shipping. He can sound more kass'aq than kass'aq when he wants to."

Maybe that's why people steer clear of him, Joseph thought. The Nicholais, despite their economic success, weren't exactly respected in the village. Ordinary hunters and fishermen, people who brought in big moose in the fall, or who netted tons of fish in the summer, were the ones everybody looked up to. They shared what they gleaned from the land, as tradition demanded. It seemed like the Nicholais only took. "Does he ever do anything besides work?" Joseph asked. "You know—hunting, fishing, trapping?"

"Hmm . . . not much, I guess. Just girls in the family, and no one to train," Elena replied. "Plus the store keeps him busy every day except Sunday." No one hunted or fished on Sunday.

Joseph hoped working at the store wouldn't keep him half that busy. They turned a corner, and there sat the store, just slightly larger than a regular house but freshly painted a deep maroon and marked with a professionally painted sign, added just a few months before, announcing its presence to the occasional visiting outsider.

The smell of new rubber mud boots mixed with the tangy scent of a few weathered oranges and the full aroma of ground coffee greeted them as they entered the store. The scent of a freshly mopped floor topped off the conglomeration of smells.

Nicholai's store was not much like the two big supermarkets in Bainbridge. There were no refrigerator or freezer sections, just aisles of canned and dry goods, with brands that had been the mainstay of village life for decades: Sunny Jim jam, Sailor Boy pilot bread, Krusteaz pancake mix. A few items ordered by mistake had gathered a thick layer of dust as they sat on the shelves—detergent for automatic dishwashers in a place where no one had running water and shaving cream in a place where men had little if any facial hair. Apparently Mr. Nicholai hadn't mastered the ordering and return process at the time those items had come in.

The store owner sat in his office, his stout body and graying hair visible through a plate-glass window that gave him a view over the counter and the cashier. Joseph had seen him keep a close eye on all transactions from there. At the moment he was engaged in a heated discussion on the telephone. His words were inaudible, but his bushy eyebrows rose and fell over his dark eyes, and his mouth opened wide as if making the full sounds of kass'aq words. Joseph and Elena stood outside the open doorway and waited for him to finish.

Someone just slightly larger than Joseph, dressed as he was in flannels and jeans, came backing down the stairway that led to the storeroom above, hunched over with the weight of two large boxes he was carrying. He set the boxes on the floor at the foot of the stairs, lifted an arm to wipe his forehead, and turned to look Joseph square in the eye.

Great, Joseph thought, it's Henry. Just like at the community center the other night, Joseph instantly felt the old family tension associated with his cousin. Though it had never been explained to him, Joseph had felt the undercurrents of this tension whenever village gatherings transpired. Whether it was a potlatch after someone's death, a feast after a wedding, or a full-blown celebration like Slaviq, the Russian Orthodox

Christmas, Joseph's mother always herded her brood to the far side of the room if Henry Alexie and his family were there.

Evidently the feud went way back, because Grandfather didn't speak to or about Henry's family, either. In fact, Joseph couldn't remember any words that had ever been spoken between the adults of the two families. When their paths had crossed at school, the boys had carried on the same cold distance between them. Henry always appeared to Joseph to be surly and not very smart. Joseph hoped that if he got the store job it wouldn't require much mingling with his cousin.

The clatter of the phone receiver in its cradle got Joseph's attention. "Ten percent for shipping," Mr. Nicholai growled under his breath. "They'll put me under yet."

He looked up and saw his eldest daughter first. "Elena," he said. His lips curved almost to a smile. "And how was school?"

"Fine, Dad. I've brought Joseph—remember?" Elena's eyes shone bright under the heavy blue shadow on her eyelids. She turned and lightly pushed Joseph forward.

Joseph nodded respectfully at Mr. Nicholai and looked down, waiting to be spoken to.

"Well, Elena tells me you'd like a job. What can you do?" Mr. Nicholai asked, raising an eyebrow and shuffling some papers at his desk.

Joseph looked up and tried not to mumble. "I'm strong and I work hard. I'm always carrying and lifting for my grandfather and my mom."

"Yes, I suppose you are," Mr. Nicholai said, in a voice

less gruff than Joseph had ever heard from him. Something about this tone of voice set Joseph on edge. We don't want your pity, he wished he could say, just because my mother was young and foolish, marrying that kass'aq and thinking he could settle in the village for the rest of his life. At least she had been strong enough to stay in the village with her family when he left.

Mr. Nicholai cleared his throat and spoke more gruffly. "I suppose we could try you out—after school, until closing each day. You can stock and sweep. Elena will show you where everything is." The decision made, he turned back to his papers.

Joseph's heart fluttered and sank as he followed after Elena. It was a job. He would have money to pay off the debt and, with that many hours, perhaps some to spare. But every day—he surely wouldn't be able to play on the basketball team or wrestle in the winter. And he'd have to do his trapping in the dark or on weekends. He could hardly ask for fewer hours, though, on his very first day. Maybe later, if things worked out, he could ask to work less, or maybe pay ahead on the debt and quit.

"Thanks," Joseph said softly. Mr. Nicholai didn't acknowledge that he had heard. Elena touched Joseph's arm and led him to the back room, where she pointed out the location of his time card and the broom.

"So, I guess that's all you'll need to get started," she said with a smile.

Joseph nodded. The door creaked open and in came Henry. He took a long look at Joseph, then turned to Elena.

"He working here now?" Henry asked her.

"Starting tomorrow," Elena replied steadily.

Joseph shifted his weight and found himself hoping again that his path would seldom cross Henry's at the store. He turned to face Elena directly. "Well, I'll be going now," Joseph said. As he reached for the door, Elena closed in behind him.

"I promised Dad I'd stay and help him with the books," Elena whispered as the door shut behind them. "But I don't want to get left in the same room with Henry," she added with an exaggerated shudder.

"See you later, then," Joseph said. "Thanks again for helping with your dad."

Joseph savored the leisure of the walk home, realizing as he went that he would seldom get to enjoy the village in daylight after his job started tomorrow. And, once he got home, he would have to explain his decision to his mother without revealing all the circumstances that were compelling him to work.

In fact, Joseph spent the first few hours of the evening at home absorbed in his thoughts, trying to decide exactly what to say to Anna. Finally, after the others had settled into bed, Joseph moved over to the table and took a seat across from his mom.

Anna was beading a border for a parka she had made to order for Mrs. Kingston. Beading had always seemed a painstaking task to Joseph. His mother sat hunched over, squinting at the tiny beads that rolled around on saucers, poking with her thin needle at the even tinier holes.

"Mom, maybe you need glasses," Joseph said.

103

"Iii, perhaps," Anna replied without looking up from her task.

"And you're always working. Why don't you take a break and relax once in awhile?" Joseph asked. Immediately, though, he regretted not what he had said but how he had said it. He hadn't meant it as a criticism.

Fortunately, his mother looked up with a half smile. "Relax?" she said. "I do, sometimes. You know I have tea with Hannah almost every day. That's relaxing, for me."

Joseph returned the half smile and shook his head. It didn't seem much like relaxing, not compared to all the time she spent cooking, cleaning, sewing, and tending the younger ones.

Anna set down her beading and rubbed both eyes with the palms of her hands. "Besides," she said, "these parkas and hats that I make pay for your food and clothes, you know—except for the checks."

Joseph knew the details of her thoughts. The checks from his father couldn't always be counted on. Anna and Mike had never officially divorced, so there was no court-mandated child support, only what Mike chose to send, when he chose to send it. A few years ago, the checks had dwindled to almost nothing, and while they had come with increasing regularity in the past few months, he knew Anna couldn't trust this distant person to provide for them.

"I've been thinking," Joseph said slowly, "that I could get a job. You know—pay for some of my own clothes and things. Maybe get some better basketball shoes . . ." Joseph's voice trailed off. He hoped he didn't sound too ungrateful.

His mother shook her head. "No, Joseph," she said. "You don't need to get a job. Enjoy your high school years while you can, and learn, so you can do well in life. There's time for work later."

It was just what Joseph had feared she would say. "I've already spoken with Mr. Nicholai, Mom," he said. "He told me I could start tomorrow, stocking shelves and cleaning."

Anna turned back to her work, picking now at several of the light blue beads. It seemed to Joseph that an eternity of silence passed between them.

"Well, then, I guess you have a job," she said at last, without looking up.

Joseph leaned back in his chair and glanced around the corner at Sam, looking so small and vulnerable beneath the blankets on his bed. A wistful feeling swept over him. To be so young again that you could climb into your mother's lap when everything went wrong, and she could stroke your hair and hold you tight and whisper that everything would be fine. But those days were long gone.

TEN

THUS JOSEPH STARTED A NEW ROUTINE of school, work, and chores at home. It seemed he was forever lifting, pushing, pulling, or carrying something. He found his forearms and biceps growing thick and tough, and he grimaced at the thought that he might have no chance to use these bulging muscles on the wrestling mats this year. Most nights he would fall into bed as soon as the water hauling and driftwood chopping were complete, relaxing at last into the darkness of a hard and dreamless sleep.

At the store, his routine was also steady and hard. He would hurry over immediately after school, while Simon and the others made off for basketball practice in the gym. Once at the store, he would carry box after box from the storeroom, taking care not to bump into Henry, who was usually engaged in the same task.

One time, not long after his job began, Joseph had started bounding up the stairs, not looking where he was going. Henry had been backing down, his arms loaded with boxes, and the two collided. They wavered a moment, finally catching their balance, but the boxes had gone flying. Fortunately they contained rolls of paper towels, and they landed flat on the floor without knocking any cans or jars off the shelves.

"Stay out of my way, you fool," Henry had snarled at Joseph. "Do you see how much damage you could have done, not to mention almost knocking me down these stairs?" He clenched his fists, and Joseph's eyes widened. Then Henry stomped down the steps to retrieve his load. After that, Joseph worked even harder to avoid his cousin, and they exchanged nothing but steely glares whenever they did happen to meet.

Mr. Nicholai was as gruff as ever, so Elena, who stopped by nearly every day, became a bright spot in Joseph's routine. She always had a smile and some news to share with him. When the news was some of her mother's trashy gossip, Joseph would pull away into serious labor in the storeroom, but when she talked of school or her favorite shows or, better yet, asked about his trapping plans, Joseph responded with a small smile and a few words of his own.

Once he even let her know how much he missed being on the basketball team this year. It was right before the team's first game, when they would travel by charter plane to play Apaniak, a coastal village about forty minutes away by air.

"But Joseph," Elena had said, "you would be one of the best scorers on the team. You played so well at the grade school. Everyone's been asking why you haven't gone out. Do you really have to work this much?"

Joseph had swallowed hard and nodded. "I do wish I was playing, more than you could know," he admitted.

"Couldn't you just work on Saturdays?" Elena suggested.

And pay fifty dollars every two weeks? Joseph kept these words inside, of course. Aloud he said, "Well, I'm trying to save up enough to get my mom one of those commercial skin-sewing machines for Christmas. They're kind of expensive."

"Gee, all for your mom," Elena commented, clearly impressed.

Joseph swallowed his guilt and told himself it wasn't exactly a lie. He especially didn't like lying to close friends like Elena and Simon, but he had to tell them some story about why he had this sudden urge to earn money. He still hoped that he could pull off paying for both the sewing machine and the debt. But that hope grew dimmer with every paycheck, when he saw how much the government took for taxes and how many hours it took to top fifty dollars of net pay every two weeks.

From the windows of the school and the windows of the store, Joseph watched the days go by. Autumn passed quickly into winter, as it did every year in the Kuskokwim Delta. The stark white snow geese and tundra swans, the green-necked mallards and green-winged teals had long since ceased to cackle overhead, and only the occasional caw of a solitary raven broke the windswept silence of ice and snow.

The snow beckoned to Joseph, for winter was the time for setting snares and traps to catch lush, furbearing mammals fattened for winter: beaver, land otter, and mink. But his cycle of work and school had left time for little else. By the time most Saturdays came around, he was too weary to pull himself from bed in time to take advantage of the shrinking hours of daylight.

Besides, the old snow-go wouldn't run properly after sitting all summer in the wind and rain. He could pull it to a start, but it would cough, sputter, and die within seconds. Finally, in the waning daylight of one Saturday in mid-November, Joseph pulled off the hood and set to the carburetor with a wrench. Before long, he heard the crunch of snow underfoot and looked up to see Sam standing beside the snow machine.

"Watcha doing, Joseph?" his brother asked, pulling at the thumbs of his mittens.

"Just trying to get this hunk of junk to run for more than three seconds at a time," Joseph growled. He removed a glove and pulled out a spark plug to see if it was fouled.

Sam didn't speak as Joseph turned his attention to the machine, but Joseph could feel his brother's eyes on him as he watched the entire trial-and-error process. Before long, Sam was stomping his feet and shifting his weight back and forth. The north wind blew hard, and the angled sun did nothing to warm the air.

Joseph stopped his tinkering and looked up at his red-cheeked brother. "You go in now," he said, resting a hand on Sam's shoulder. "You can learn this on a warmer day."

Sam wiped at his nose with his coat sleeve and nodded. Then he ran back to the house like a lead dog who had just spied the finish line at the end of a big race.

Joseph closed the hood with a clatter and gave the rope a hard pull. The engine putt-putted slowly at first, but when Joseph put his thumb to the throttle and revved it, it roared. Success at last. With one thumb still on the throttle, he used his free arm to lift up the back end of the machine. The track spun, throwing off chunks of snow and ice.

Joseph straddled the seat and took off down the trail through the village, past the Nicholais', past the grade school, along the river, beyond the store, over to the high school, and then back along the airstrip. Cold wind stung his cheeks and made his eyes water, but Joseph didn't mind. It was enough to ride free and fast, as if he didn't have a care in the world.

At the airstrip, Joseph brought his machine to a stop and hit the kill switch. A twinge of regret ran through him as he looked at the spot where the lopsided plane had sat, but he pushed the regret aside and looked beyond to where the frozen tundra beckoned. The trail went on as far as the eye could see across the flat winterscape. Follow it, and you would eventually hit the wide Kuskokwim River, which soon would be frozen so solid that not just snow machines but trucks could use it for a winter highway.

From there you could pick up a river like the Kwethluk and follow it toward the Kilbuck Mountains, home of the legendary little people, who walked mostly in the spirit world but sometimes used their magic on hapless humans. All kinds of furbearing mammals lived there, too—lynx, bear, wolverine, and even wolves.

Not that there weren't plenty of furbearers on the nearby tundra. Plump beaver tunneled in and out of the sloughs and rivers all winter long, along with silky brown Kuskokwim mink. Joseph had set snares and traps for both during many winters, starting when he was not much older than Sam, under his grandfather's watchful eye. But this year, where was the time? Joseph took a last wistful look at the wide open space before him, then pulled his machine to a start and drove in a wide circle back to the village. Soon, he hoped, he would be able to make time to venture onto the tundra and get his trapping underway.

Before Joseph knew it, Thanksgiving was upon them. Thanksgiving was no great celebration in the village, not like Christmas or Slaviq. Still, his mother pulled a goose from the freezer and roasted it instead of boiling it. With the savory bird, she fixed canned corn and mashed potatoes.

Grandfather joined them for the meal. They feasted until they couldn't hold another bit; all of them, including Sam, cleaned up the meat from each bone as they had been taught. His grandfather and mother even sucked the marrow from the bones on their plates, but that was one tradition Joseph had never picked up. For dessert, Anna had whipped together Crisco, sugar, and berries for *akutaq*, the traditional Eskimo ice cream. Each spoonful slid down Joseph's throat, and the shortening made him feel warm to the tips of his toes, not at all like kass'aq ice cream, which always made him shiver.

"Delicious, Anna," Grandfather said to his daughter. He leaned back in the chair and took a long drink from his mug of tea.

"Quyana," Joseph's mother replied, giving thanks for

the compliment. She shifted in her seat and fingered a beaded earring that dangled from one ear. "I ate too much, though."

Joseph felt uncomfortably full himself. He had never gotten used to the American tradition of gorging oneself on Thanksgiving. It ran contrary to so much that he had been taught as a child about not being greedy. Everyone knew the story of the boy who ate everything he killed instead of bringing it home to his grandmother, who was starving as he was. That bloated boy could not become a man until his grandmother cut him open and released all the animals for everyone to eat.

Joseph's eyes drifted to the TV. For once, the children weren't gathered to watch; he could hear Dora and Elsie in the back room—playing school, of all things. He couldn't understand Dora, especially—one minute she was winking at a boy, and the next she was playing make-believe. Sam was spinning a toy truck across the floor, delighting in its high-impact collisions with the wall.

From the television, the roar of the crowd mingled with the sportscaster's play-by-play as a Lions player intercepted a pass and ran for thirty yards, or something to that effect. No one played football in the village, and Joseph feigned only mild interest in the sport.

From above the TV, the CB crackled to life: "B-two-nine, this is C-C-five. Over."

Anna rose to take the call. "Roger, C-C-five, this is B-two-nine. Go ahead," she said into the set.

"Phone call for Joseph," the CB voice responded. The Benchleys were one of only a handful of families in the village who still used the community center phone instead of running a line directly to their home.

"Roger," Anna said flatly. "Just a minute."

She looked at Joseph, and he shook his head. Who would be calling him but his father? It had happened before—three, maybe four times so far this year. But just to be sure, Joseph said, "Ask who it is."

Anna relayed the question, and the reply crackled back, "Mike Benchley."

"No way," Joseph said. He knew his mother neither expected nor encouraged any other answer. It was like a pact between them, this distance they kept from the man who had let them both down.

"Tell him Joseph's not available," Anna relayed to the community center operator.

"Roger," came the reply. A long pause followed; then the voice returned. "He says he'd like to speak to Dora and Elsie then."

"One minute," Anna said. She stepped toward the back room, the CB transmitter still in her hand, but Dora had already stuck her head around the corner.

"Somebody wants to talk to me?" she asked eagerly.

"You and Elsie, too. It's your father again," Anna explained. Dora's face beamed.

"Elsie, it's Dad," she called to her sister. "Come on!"

The girls dashed from the back room and were already wiggling into their boots and coats as Anna gave word to the operator: "Roger. They're on their way. Over and out."

"Roger. Over and out," the operator said dully.

The door slammed behind the two girls before Anna had even returned to her seat.

Anna took a long drink of tea and stared out the window. After a moment, she spoke.

"Ila-i," she said. "I hope this is not asking for trouble, letting the girls talk with him so freely."

Joseph was quick to reply. "Everything about him is trouble. He thinks it's so easy—just call once in awhile, or send a check, and everything's all right."

"Yes, but you know how excited the girls get over him calling, especially when he went for so many years without doing it," Anna said.

"And he could decide tomorrow never to call again. Then how will they feel? Better to cut the whole business off before they get hurt," Joseph said. Then he lowered his voice. "Besides, what about Sam? Don't you think he wonders why Dad never asks to talk with him?"

Anna shrugged her shoulders. "I can't help it if your father left before he knew I was expecting Sam. Someday the girls will say something about him, I'm sure."

Joseph shook his head. "I don't know, Mom," he said. "Their heads are so full of themselves, I doubt they'll ever think to mention him." Joseph lowered his voice even more. "And Sam—he's better off not knowing he has a father."

"Akleng!" Grandfather said. He sat up and leaned toward Joseph. "Your father is your father. Part of who he is cannot be helped. Someday he may change. Who can say? You owe him a certain loyalty."

"Loyalty to a kass'aq?" Joseph said. It came out as almost a hiss.

"Loyalty to your father, no matter who he is," his grandfather said firmly.

Joseph felt a thousand angry words jostle inside, but

he said absolutely nothing. He looked over at his mother. Her face was without expression, as if none of this talk had anything to do with her. Grandfather leaned back in his chair. Joseph couldn't remember ever feeling anger toward his grandfather, but he felt it now. He felt angry with everything and everyone, most of all with his unseen father.

Pushing his chair from the table, Joseph got up and flopped onto the bed by the TV. He stared blankly at the screen, listening to the grunts and slams as the players collided. He felt like shoving and hitting someone himself. Maybe this wasn't such a bad sport after all, even if there was no point to it. He concentrated harder on the screen, willing himself to become lost in a game that he didn't understand.

ELEVEN

IT WAS MORE THAN A WEEK LATER that Joseph finally made good on his resolve to get out early on a Saturday and set some snares. He rose at the regular schooltime, while daylight was just a promise beyond the horizon. He ate his pilot bread and drank a strong cup of tea in silence, listening only to the rhythm of sleep from the rest of the family in the other room.

At last he would breathe the fresh winter air and challenge himself with the setting of snares for beaver along the same trapline he had followed for the past three years—the line that had been his grandfather's, generously shared with his father, and finally passed down to Joseph. He wouldn't be able to put out as many snares as he had last year, but at least he could get out a few to bring dark red beaver meat to the table and supplement his income by selling a pelt or two.

Joseph downed the last gulp of lukewarm tea and pulled on his insulted coveralls. One by one he gathered his snares and reached for his .22. He took a final look around and moved into the porch, where he found a shovel, ice chisel, and ax. All of these he put into a weathered wooden sled that sat outside, and he attached the sled to the hitch on the back of his snow machine.

The machine showed its age, with a faded cowling and torn seat, but it purred to a start with the adjustments Joseph had made. He lifted the machine and hit the throttle to spin the packed snow from the track. It roared with power and thick exhaust in the morning quiet.

Joseph sat on the machine and set it in motion. He steered cautiously at first, over the bumps in the narrow path that led out from the village and onto the river. Once he was on the smooth, wide river trail, he opened it up. The shrubs, willows, and drifts became a blur as he increased his speed, and the cold air stung his cheeks and caused his eyes to water. He felt a sense of exhilaration and power at being able to travel at these speeds. A traditional dog team would have been quieter but not nearly as efficient; no one used dogs anymore except for racing.

About two miles from the village, Joseph broke from the main trail and headed off toward Nervik Lake, where he would set his first snares. His eyes strained at the landmarks: a tiny hillock to the left, a narrow slough to the right, and ahead an edging of snow-covered willows that signaled a larger body of water. A stranger could never have found his way in this snow-covered landscape, Joseph thought with satisfaction. Under its cloak of winter white, the tundra was more barren and desolate than in any other season.

Finally, Nervik Lake loomed ahead, a vast expanse of frozen white set off by a fringe of waist-high willows. Joseph slowed to a stop and hit the kill switch. He sat a moment, savoring the sudden quiet. He squinted into the slanted sunlight, which just now had begun to edge past the horizon. His eyes moved methodically around the lake as he scouted for signs of a beaver house.

On the far side, he spotted a hill of twigs, wood, and dried mud, camouflaged by snow but still visible to his trained eye. He pulled the starter cord and drove toward it, making his own trail across the windswept snow. A few feet from the beaver house, Joseph shut off his machine. From the sled, he pulled the shovel and the long-handled ice chisel.

A beaver house was like an iceberg. The haphazard collection of sticks on the surface hinted at a much larger dwelling under the ice. Joseph walked around the mound and selected two spots, one on either side, which he hoped were covering entrances to the beaver house. These would be fruitful locations for snares.

He began to shovel the snow away, down about eight inches to the ice beneath. It was easy shoveling this early in the season, but only one storm between now and the time he checked the snares could blow in enough hard-packed snow to make this portion of the process three times as difficult when he returned to check the snares.

When his shovel scraped against the ice, he traded it for the long-handled ice chisel and began a slow, rhythmic chipping, up and down, up and down, until his muscles ached with the effort. Water bubbled to the surface as a reward, and then he felt encouraged to keep chopping, widening the hole until it was a foot across and two feet long.

By now the sun had come up as far as it would on this winter day, casting light in long angles from its perch just a bit above the horizon. It would not climb across the sky as it did in the summer, but would form a short, lazy arc there on the edge of the sky, and set again within a few hours.

Even so, Joseph felt no sense of urgency. He sat back against the snow bank and breathed in deep, examining the snaring hole he had made. The air was crisp and cool in his lungs, the sun too weak to warm the winter air even though no clouds stood in its way. He wished he had thought to bring a thermos of hot tea. The steaming liquid would feel good sliding down his throat. Still, his blood coursed in his veins from the exertion of shoveling and chopping, and he was warm to the tips of his fingers.

The next task was to chop a stick to hold each snare, which Joseph did using the ax from his sled. The sticks came right off the top of the beaver house. Poor animals, Joseph thought—the same sticks they had gathered furiously last summer to build their home would now bring death to some. In his mind, he said a short thank you to the beavers, in advance, for so generously offering themselves to him.

Joseph hung a single snare from each stick and then plunged his chisel to the bottom of the hole to gauge the depth. The plunge revealed a shallow spot a little over two feet deep. He adjusted the snares to hang a foot above the bottom and settled three in a row into the hole, the sticks bridging across the gap.

After splashing water on the end of each stick to freeze and hold it firmly in place, Joseph moved his operation to the far side of the house and repeated the process. There the water was a bit deeper, and he adjusted the snares accordingly, setting three as he had in the first spot, imagining all the while the fat beavers gliding through the icy water below, hopefully following the path he had envisioned with the placement of his snares.

The cold began to edge through the felt liners of his boots. The sun hung at its meager peak, and Joseph calculated the time. He could still head for Igayik Lake, where every year several beavers built their homes. He looked over his work on the set. Overall, it was inconspicuous, and Joseph was pleased.

He returned to his machine, the dry snow crunching loudly beneath his boots, and replaced the tools he had used. Gunning the snow-machine engine, he set off, breaking trail across the tundra. As he rode, he felt like the rodeo cowboys he had seen on TV, bucked about by the frozen tussocks and countless dips in the winter-locked land, and he smiled at himself over this unusual image: an Eskimo cowboy.

Before long, Igayik Lake came into view, an even vaster expanse of white than Nervik Lake. As Joseph's machine dipped over the land's edge and onto the ice, overflow water rose up and covered its track. It was still early in the season, Joseph reminded himself; a lake this size might not be frozen solid yet.

Going through the ice brought death to a few careless snow-machine travelers on the delta every year. Joseph would not be one of them. He veered the machine back toward shore and skirted the lake on land, searching for more telltale signs of beaver. Finally, he spotted a beaver house twice the size of the one he had just visited.

He pulled the machine up close and walked around the mound of sticks. The under-ice dwelling must be the size of a small sod house of the type his ancestors had built, he realized. The likely spots for entrances to this house seemed obvious to Joseph, and the delight of possibly catching several beaver awakened his senses. He shoveled and chopped, setting out six more snares. While he worked, he calculated. He already had some extra money stashed away from his checks, left over after he made his payments. If beaver pelts fetched a good price this season, perhaps that sewing machine could find its way to their kitchen table after all.

When Joseph had made and filled each snare hole, he leaned back against his machine to catch his breath, which was still heavy from the shoveling. He surveyed the lake, frozen and still in the November wind, and he twinged with the memory of the last time he had been here, his chance at a fat goose taken by the white-haired teacher.

Joseph's fury was dim now. It had been overshadowed by hot embarrassment at the story he had told. Elena, thank heavens, had stayed on his side, though he wasn't quite sure why. He suspected she knew that it was the teacher who told the truth, but she hadn't seemed to hold it against Joseph. For this he was grateful, and he vowed to be honest with her and with others from now on.

As for the teacher—well, the truce continued. Joseph still despised his kass'aq ways: his smell, his voice, his direct manner that stood in sharp contrast with the Yup'ik people, the Real People. But at least he hadn't tried to make himself Eskimo like the teachers sometimes did, wearing colored *qaspeqs* and stuttering sad attempts at Yup'ik words. Mr. Townsend kept to himself for the most part. And the transactions with Fish and Game on Joseph's behalf were discreet. Joseph was grateful for this small favor, though he hated the feeling of obligation that now bound him to this white man.

Mr. Townsend was pulling their class through *Romeo and Juliet* these days. Joseph found himself strangely captivated by the Shakespearean play. Sunny Verona was certainly a distant world from the windswept tundra, Joseph thought as he surveyed the familiar landscape. But the feud between the Capulets and the Montagues reminded him of the tension between his own family and Henry Alexie's, and the bloody sword fights brought back stories his grandfather told about Eskimo groups that warred with spears. The love part— well, he wasn't so sure about that. But he liked the language—rhythmic and lilting, more like Yup'ik than modern-day American English, with its flat vowels and twangs.

Enough daydreaming, Joseph told himself. He had a job to get to. With the increased business of holiday shopping, Mr. Nicholai had scheduled Joseph for a few hours on Saturdays, beginning today. He started up the machine and headed back toward the village, following his previous trail. He focused on finding the path, not wanting to stray too far. It was easy to hit a slough with a bit of unfrozen current, or even to lose your way before reaching sight of the village.

The village was just looming into view when he came upon a huge flock of ptarmigan. There must have been nearly fifty of the birds, all white against the snow except for the brown tips of their feathers. Those, too, would eventually turn white when the fullness of winter set in. They huddled together just off the trail on a patch of tundra blown almost bare by the wind. Joseph killed the engine and crept off his machine, pulling his .22 from the sled and slinging it over his shoulder.

He moved slowly, each step tempered, toward the birds. Though the snow crunched underfoot, the birds continued to peck undisturbed at the frozen tundra, with only an occasional raucous cackle rising from within the flock. As long as he could get within shooting range without raising a general call of alarm, Joseph knew he could bring a few birds home for dinner.

Within moments, he was able to raise his gun and aim. The shot rang into the distance, and the flock scattered, leaving one bird lying on the ground, a tiny scarlet pool forming beneath its breast. He picked up the limp body by its large, downy feet and sneaked back toward the flock, which had resettled only fifty yards away. This time he was able to get off two shots and was rewarded with two more warm, fresh birds. The meat would be rich and dark in their soup that night.

The first bird, he resolved, would go to Grandfather. He longed to stay and continue shooting, to fill the freezer and delight his mother, but the dropping sun signaled that the afternoon was closing in. He needed to be at work by three-thirty. Reluctantly, he set the three birds in his sled and resumed the journey home.

A smile lit Grandfather's face when Joseph burst through his door with the bird. *"Quyana,"* he said. "You are a fine hunter."

"Next week, there will be beaver, too. I can't stay now, though. Do you think you can pluck it yourself?" Joseph eyed his grandfather's gnarled hands.

"Iii. If not, I'll call Dora on the CB."

"Good idea. She needs something to keep her busy. See you later!" Joseph was already backing out the door.

Another minute on the snow machine took him to his own front porch. He dropped his gear there and brought the remaining birds inside. "Mom, here's dinner," he called out. He held them up for her to see, then set them before her on the table, beside the bright red calico she had spread out for cutting a *qaspeq*.

"Look, Joseph. You got a letter." Elsie, on her knees, bounced up and down as she said it, and the bed springs rang. She pointed to the table.

There, near where he had set the ptarmigan, was an envelope addressed to him: *Mr. Joseph Benchley*. A tiny streak of blood from the birds had smeared across it and was already turning brown, but that didn't obscure the postmark: Portland, Oregon.

The combination of anger, hurt, and pride that he felt whenever his father tried to reach him by phone rose quickly within Joseph. So his father thought he could cajole him with written words now. Joseph snatched up the letter and glanced at the clock: 3:20.

"I've got to go to work, Mom," he said. Elsie watched,

wide-eyed, as he dashed to the bedroom, kicking off his boots and pulling off his coveralls as he went.

"Aren't you going to open it?" his sister asked.

Joseph shoved the letter in his top dresser drawer, crumpling it beside a soapstone seal and an envelope stuffed with spare change and a few larger bills. Then he flew from the room and out of the house, grabbing his nylon parka from the porch, without answering his sister's question.

His feet pounded the boardwalk as he ran toward the store. The snow machine was useless among the maze of boardwalks in the village, so he had to rely on his legs. Joseph was pleased that he still ran fast, even without the conditioning of basketball.

He bounded through the door at 3:30 exactly. Joseph caught his breath, hung up his coat, and pulled on his work gloves. Now he was stuck at the store until six o'clock, pulling down boxes and cramming the holiday load of merchandise onto the shelves. All kinds of new items had come in for Christmas: shiny metallic toy cars, baby dolls plastered with eternal smiles, plastic guns and holsters, noisy rattles, warm flannel shirts and wool socks, stylish sweatshirts with far-off college names stitched across the chest, and bags and bags of foil-wrapped chocolates, tiny peppermint sticks, and ribboned hard candy.

As Joseph stocked, he heard the cash register beep and ring in a flurry of sales that brought a smile even to Mr. Nicholai's gruff face. The stout man pulled himself from his desk behind the window and wandered the aisles of his little empire, mingling with the folks he'd known all his life, though he was always somehow elevated in his role as village entrepreneur.

Joseph watched the storekeeper's bushy eyebrows spring to life as the fast flow of Yup'ik words was punctuated by an occasional hearty laugh. Too bad the old man can't be so charming every day, Joseph thought. Then he felt bad for being critical. At least Mr. Nicholai had consented to the job.

He did seem to favor Henry, though. Joseph looked up from the box he was unpacking and eyed his fellow worker, who stood now at the till, entrusted with monetary transactions that had until recently been handled primarily by the Nicholai family and a few longtime employees. Henry caught his eye and glared back. A scowl formed under the hint of a scraggly mustache that darkened Henry's face, and Joseph looked away.

Joseph worked daily at keeping his distance from his cousin and managed to avoid overt conflict. But Joseph could feel his resentment rise as he heaved and stacked, getting sweaty and dirty, while Henry stood nonplussed at the till. To Joseph, he seemed like the occasional mean and lazy sled dog who liked to nip at the heels of the others but then slacked in the harness and let them do the work.

Finally closing time came. Mr. Nicholai dimmed the lights and plodded upstairs to check the progress in the storeroom. No longer needed at the till, Henry pulled himself away and, with a push broom, began the final sweep of the floors, starting at the far end, by the stairs. He pushed in long, slow strokes, letting the dust settle between each one. Joseph retrieved the smaller broom from Mr. Nicholai's office and set out at a brisker pace, starting at the office doorway. His stomach was growling, and he longed for the full taste of ptarmigan soup in his mouth, so he swept with energy, anxious to close up for the day and get home.

Joseph angled the broom around the counter which held the till. As he tucked the bristles between the lower edge of the counter and the floor, the broom caught on something. Joseph pushed again with the broom and bent down to see what he had unearthed. It was a twenty-dollar bill. Joseph picked it up and shook off the dust.

He glanced up. Henry was focused on the slow push of his broom across the store. Mr. Nicholai was not in sight. Twenty dollars—not a fortune, but it would add to Joseph's fund. His heart leapt at the thought of stashing it with the other leftover cash in his top dresser drawer.

Still, Joseph reasoned with himself, he could hardly pretend that the bill had no owner. He had found it on the till side of the counter, which made it clearly part of Mr. Nicholai's abundant catch of the day. Joseph sighed lightly. He had watched enough to know how to open the register. He punched a button and, with a quiet *ding*, the drawer flung open.

Joseph lifted the arm from the other twenty-dollar bills and slid his find on top. With a gentle click, he shut the register drawer and looked up for his broom. His eyes met Henry's, glaring again from across the room. Joseph shook his head and resumed sweeping. The guy does nothing but glare, he thought, and now he's probably mad that I've touched his precious till. So, let him be mad.

It was not until late that night, when his belly was warm and full with ptarmigan soup and the rest of the family had snuggled under the covers in their tiny bedroom, that Joseph decided to pull the letter from his dresser drawer. He smoothed the envelope across the edge of the table and listened to the wind whistle down the stovepipe. The house was shaking ever so slightly on its pilings. A storm was moving in.

Joseph's fingers shook ever so slightly, too, as he tore open the envelope. From it he pulled a single sheet of notebook paper, filled with neatly penned script:

Dear Joseph,

I understand, after all these years, why you might not want to talk with me on the phone. But I got to thinking how old you must be now, and that maybe I could write to you.

Well, it's hard to know where to start. I wish I had even a picture of you and your sisters to let me know how you are now. The only one I have was taken years ago, when you were eight. I still remember your smile and how you would listen and learn from your grandfather. I think you did much better than I did.

It took many years for me to make a life for myself here after those years in the village. I felt for so long like I was caught between two worlds and would never fit into either one. Sometimes I thought of coming back, but then I remembered all the reasons why it hadn't worked. Besides,

I haven't had much money. It's done me some good to know that what little I've had, I've shared with your mom. She's a good woman, though I suppose she doesn't think much of me now.

Perhaps you don't, either. Still, Joseph, I'd like to know you. I'd like you to know me, for whatever I'm worth. Now I've started saving a little extra money, set aside to buy a plane ticket. Do you think you would like to come and spend a few weeks with me in Portland this summer? It's a nice place, really, and we could see a movie, go to the beach, drive up to Seattle for a Mariners game. It rains a lot here, but then you'd be used to that.

Think about it. You don't have to let me know right away.

Love,
Dad

Love, Dad. The two words didn't seem to fit together. Joseph felt his heart thumping with anger as he reread the letter. Then he pushed the paper aside. The old resentment flooded back in, and Joseph allowed it to lap at the recesses of his mind, filling him completely.

Go visit his dad in Portland this summer? Absolutely not. Joseph crammed the letter back into its envelope. He stepped to the stove and, with a fork, lifted the lid of one burner. He dangled the envelope above the flame that burned brightly inside.

But something welled up in his throat, and he dropped the lid back with a clatter. Instead, he shoved the envelope back in the top dresser drawer and thrust himself angrily beneath the covers. There he listened to the sighs of the wind as they echoed lonely in the night.

TWELVE

WHEN JOSEPH OPENED HIS EYES the next morning, his body felt tired and his nerves on edge. He lay on his back for a moment and listened. TV sounds came from the other room, and the wind still howled around the outside walls. Looking about, he saw only crumpled sheets and blankets on the other beds, and a thin gray light filtered through the curtains. Somewhere beyond the storm the sun was shining, he thought. He guessed the time to be around ten o'clock, but he still felt exhausted.

There had been the dream again, where he was part of a pack, chasing the shadowy man from the village. And just like before, the roles had switched in his dream, and Joseph found himself running from the villagers instead of chasing with them. He shoved the leftover hot fear of pursuit to the back of his mind and sat up.

At least it was Sunday, a day of relative freedom, with only water to haul and buckets to dump and the obligation of church to attend. But as he peeked out the bedroom curtains, Joseph saw that the blizzard raging outside had changed his feeling of freedom to confinement. The snow swirled in sharp angles, a wall of white that blocked all vision in the morning gray. He couldn't even see the boardwalk beside the house, much less

Grandfather's house in the distance. Even church would cease to be an obligation while this storm continued.

A restless irritation tingled within him. The snares he had set yesterday were certainly buried by now under the blowing, drifting snow. He would be lucky to be able to find the sets again without a good deal of shoveling. Hopefully, the sticks of the beaver houses would still show through.

He drew the curtain and stretched his arms in front of his chest, pulling out the tightness in his biceps and across his shoulder blades. He ached with the remnants of the shoveling, chopping, lifting, and unloading from the day before. He looked around and saw clutter closing in everywhere.

"Can't anybody pick up their things?" he growled, kicking at a doll and a wadded pair of jeans that lay on the floor in his path.

Elsie and Dora looked up from the cartoon show that blared from the TV and giggled. Sam, sprawled out beside them, asked with a serious look, "What's the matter, Joseph?"

Joseph ignored the question and approached the washbasin, plunging his hands in the soapy water and drawing it up toward his face. The water stung at the corners of his eyes, and when he grabbed a towel to wipe it away, the towel smelled musty and left him feeling dingier than before he had washed.

He caught his expression in the spattered mirror above the basin and felt his dissatisfaction mount. His wavy hair stuck out in all directions, and against his pale winter face, his dark, round eyes and kass'aq nose protruded. His head looked especially thin and long today. Joseph cursed his father under his breath.

In the mirror, he could see behind him to his mother, who was kneading bread on the kitchen table. Flour smudged her face and a strand of hair that hung beside it, and she wore a stretchy pullover that had lost its shape many washings ago. Why didn't she take better care of herself? Joseph thought of all the TV moms he had seen. Even at their most frazzled, they always managed to look ten times better than this woman who was up to her elbows in flour, pushing and pulling at the sticky dough.

"Mom, they sell bread at the store, you know," Joseph said, letting the edge of irritation sweep through his voice. "We don't have to be so primitive."

"Primitive?" His mother sighed. Joseph dug through school papers, floss and needles, napkins and jars, shoving them to the edge of the table to find a knife and some butter, which he located by the bleeding grease spot forming on a half-finished essay he had been writing for school. Casting the essay to the floor, he moved the buttering operation to the cluttered counter and fixed his morning pilot bread. Then he pulled a chair away and chewed noisily at his breakfast.

The inside air stifled his breath, and he longed to be outdoors. Brushing off the crumbs, Joseph rose and pulled on his jacket, gloves, and hat. He opened the cabinet door below the washbasin and found the gray-water bucket only half full. Even after he dumped the soapy basin water in it, the water level was still far from the top, but he hoisted it up anyway. It was a good enough excuse to go a short distance in the storm.

He had to shove hard just to open the outside door, and the sharp snow stung his face. He turned against the wind to catch his breath and steadied the bucket with its sloshing water, grateful now that it was not filled to the brim. Even through his hat, the wind roared against his ears, which began to ache as he plodded carefully down the boardwalk into the storm.

There wasn't far to walk to dump a gray-water bucket; anywhere away from the house and onto the tundra would do. He calculated his steps as he walked, not wanting to pause inadvertently in front of another house that he couldn't see in the storm and dump gray water on the doorstep. Finally, fairly certain that he stood on the boardwalk midway between his grandfather's house and his own, he turned so that the wind pounded at his back and hurled the water into the storm.

Returning home was much easier. The wind pushed him along, and he had only to struggle at keeping his bearings in the swirling snow. As long as he stayed on the boardwalk, there was no real danger, but in a whiteout storm like this, a person could easily walk past his destination and end up on someone else's front porch. Joseph squinted. A splash of maroon showed faintly through the curtain of snow, and he veered to the right. Only when he actually reached the door and turned the rusty knob was he sure that he had gauged his destination correctly and was entering his own house.

Once inside the porch, he shook off the snow that clung to his hat and gloves and stomped into the house. The storm had made him feel awake and alive again, so the stomping was more for the shedding of snow than for the release of frustration. He had pushed one boot off when his mother spoke.

"Joseph, Mr. Nicholai called on the CB. He said it's urgent. You're to go up to the store right away." She spoke in soft Yup'ik tones, a gentle hush against the wind that raged outside.

"Right away? Hasn't he looked outside? I can't believe he's even at the store. It's Sunday, after all," Joseph replied, irritation inching into his voice. A tiny pool of melted snow was forming where he stood.

"He knows the weather. He said he made it to the store just fine. He's your boss. It must be important," his mother replied in the storekeeper's defense.

"Yeah, he doesn't want to miss the chance to set me straight on something, I'm sure," Joseph growled. He was puzzled and dismayed. What could be wrong? Had he not accomplished enough yesterday? Only rarely did anyone in the village work on Sundays. And in this storm . . . His irritation flooded back with full force. If he hadn't wanted to spend the day cooped up in the house, a day unpacking dusty boxes at the store, or even a few minutes listening to a lecture from Mr. Nicholai, hardly sounded more appealing.

But then again, maybe he needs me, Joseph thought. Me instead of Henry, who's probably too soft to go out in the storm. Joseph smiled to himself. A quiet day without Henry wouldn't be so bad, and he could use the money. If he did well, perhaps Mr. Nicholai would even let Joseph take over on the till the next time the store was open for business.

"OK, I'm going then," he informed his mother, and he shoved his foot back into his boot. With hat and gloves in place, he set out to brave the storm again, thankful that the wind was blowing east to west through the village, so he didn't have to fight it on the way there. Coming home would be a different story, but hopefully the blizzard would spin itself out before long.

His only worry was to calculate his way properly on the boardwalk, which was tougher now that he had a longer distance to travel. He struggled to keep his eyes focused and his senses alert as he battled the storm. Each flake of snow pummeled like a tiny bullet against his face. He took one step, then another—around the drifting snow when he could, through it when there was no other way. Eventually, he ended up on Nastasia Paniak's doorstep and realized that he had overshot the store. He took a deep breath and backtracked twenty yards into the wind.

The store was vacant except for Mr. Nicholai, seated as usual at his big desk behind the plate-glass window. Joseph shook off the snow as best he could and proceeded into the office.

"You called for me, Mr. Nicholai?" Joseph asked. The man must surely be impressed that I've come out in this storm, he thought.

"Sit down, Joseph," Mr. Nicholai commanded, and he motioned to the chair beside the desk. Joseph complied, realizing as he settled into the chair that he had never sat for any reason while on the job.

Mr. Nicholai cleared his throat and furrowed his

eyebrows. "Joseph, we have something important to discuss." Thoughts raced through Joseph's mind. A raise? More responsibility? These seemed unlikely, but then who could read the stern storekeeper? Perhaps he liked Joseph more than he had let on. Certainly his daughter must speak well of her friend. The prospect of having earned his boss's trust warmed Joseph from deep within. But why this urgency—on a Sunday, in the middle of a blizzard?

"Something happened yesterday that has caused me great concern," the storekeeper continued. He was speaking in English now, his formal business voice. His gaze fell directly on Joseph, and instinctively, Joseph looked away.

"Our till came up short—one hundred fifty dollars short, to be precise. Perhaps you didn't know, but the register tallies its own total for the day and then we check it with a count of the money in the drawer." He could have been explaining the basic working of a snow-machine engine, except that his voice was too loud and serious.

"Now, I've talked with Henry already, and he says he saw you open the till last night right after closing." Henry! Joseph felt his heart sink in his chest.

Mr. Nicholai was laying out his case carefully, slicing a stubby hand through the air with each new point. "I've never taught you to run the till or to open it even. But clearly you've made it your business to learn."

A cry rose in Joseph's throat, but he swallowed it. Mr. Nicholai continued, "I don't have real proof, of course, so I won't bring the village police into this, but it seems clear to me that you took the money. And one hundred fifty dollars is a lot of money, Joseph." He paused for effect.

Emotions raged and swirled inside Joseph. But he had put money back; he hadn't taken it. Henry—Henry must have taken the money and blamed it on him. Joseph blinked and struggled for his voice, but Mr. Nicholai continued. "So clearly I'll have to let you go. I will withhold your last paycheck, of course. From that I will recover seventy-six dollars of my loss. I expect you to pay me back the difference—seventy-four dollars— tomorrow after school. That's the least you should do, considering how I trusted you and gave you a job when you needed one."

Joseph found his voice, though trembling, at last. "But what about—" he started.

Mr. Nicholai hadn't finished. "I trusted you because Elena likes you and said you'd be a good worker. Apparently you've fooled her, too."

Joseph's eyes turned hot and aching. He shook his head and willed his voice to speak again. "But Henry—"

Again the storekeeper cut him off with a slice of his hand through the air. "I know you don't like Henry, but don't go blaming this on him. He's worked here much longer than you, and I've been able to trust him. I'm thankful he was so observant and willing to come forward when this little problem came up. Now, good-bye." Mr. Nicholai's hand waved off toward the doorway, as if he were shooing a mangy dog from his yard.

Joseph felt too limp and heavy to rise, but somehow

he did. As he reached the doorway, he forced his head up. He would not hang his head in defeat.

Words rang in his head from another time of tension. *I must rage, even if quietly, against this untruth.* Joseph turned in the doorway, standing straight as he addressed the storekeeper.

"Mr. Nicholai." Joseph's voice was clear and firm now. "I know you may not believe me, but I want you to know. I did not take that money." With that, Joseph turned and left the store, leaving the storekeeper stroking his chin in amazement over the boy's defiant words.

Joseph's thoughts swirled like the snow around him as he struggled against the wind back toward the house. He had surprised himself there at the end, speaking up clearly on his own behalf. Part of him felt proud, and the other part ashamed at the kass'aqlike confrontation. Part of him wished he had continued in the same spirit, striding over to Henry's house and confronting him as well.

Mr. Nicholai's explanation had left no doubt that Henry had framed him, and most likely Henry was one hundred fifty dollars richer for his trouble. But there was no way to trap his cousin, at least not that Joseph could think of. He could try to spread the word that Henry had stolen the money, but the conflicting stories would meet in a frustrating dead end, and Joseph wasn't sure he had the energy. He'd been through all that before.

And Elena—what would she think? He could tell his mother and his grandfather that he'd gotten fed up and left his job, which was partly true, or he could tell them nothing and they'd probably never ask. But Elena, he knew, would already have heard from her father about her friend's shameful misconduct. He could hardly go to her door in this storm and ask to come in, to tell his version of the story.

After the incident with Mr. Townsend, she probably wouldn't believe him anyway. Joseph turned the thoughts over in his mind. Somehow, this loss hurt most of all, even more than the loss of income he would somehow have to deal with.

It was too much to consider for now. He focused on taking one step and then another, on not losing his way in the storm. Finally he reached his house. He struggled with the door and stamped the snow off his boots with empty thuds. As he stripped off his frozen wraps, he avoided his mother's questioning eyes and the children on the front-room bed. Instead, he went directly to the bedroom, and with the exhaustion that sinks in after a tremendous storm, fell into a deep sleep.

THIRTEEN

MONDAY MORNING CAME SOONER than Joseph hoped, though the hours he had spent trying to lose himself in front of the television had seemed long enough. As soon as Joseph awoke in the still darkness, he knew it was the first Monday of December, a day on which he was to hand over another fifty-dollar payment to the Fish and Game through Mr. Townsend. And now he had to turn over seventy-four dollars to Mr. Nicholai as well.

All day Sunday he had avoided scrounging in his savings drawer for the money he knew wasn't there. He had some extra, to be sure—but one hundred twenty-four dollars? It seemed unlikely. The image of the sewing machine he had hoped to purchase with the excess receded in his mind. At least now he wouldn't need to explain to Elena why he was unable to buy it—she would know. The thought of facing her added more dread to the day, and Joseph rolled over and pulled the covers up over his head.

He remembered hiding under his covers like that as a child, hoping that no one would notice that he wasn't getting up and getting ready for school. Sam did the same on some days now, and he could sometimes get away with a half hour of extra sleep before anyone noticed his absence amid the ruckus of three older ones washing, getting dressed, and gathering their packs. Eventually someone would realize that Sam was still in bed and would run in to shake him awake, and he would pull whatever clothes lay nearby over his tousled hair as his mother chided, "*Gigi, gigi*—hurry up," from the front room.

Joseph had never been able to get away with that extra half hour when he was young. As the oldest, he had been more closely watched, his presence more sorely missed. With a sigh, he flung off the covers. The soles of his feet startled as they hit the cold floor. The storm had receded late Sunday afternoon, and the mercury had dropped to ten, then twenty, then thirty below zero, according to the thermometer outside their tiny kitchen window. The oil cookstove fairly glowed with a steady burning, but in these temperatures, the heat only radiated for fifteen feet or so. That meant that the front room was warm enough, but in the bedroom, frost grew in the corners and along the baseboards of the outside walls.

Quickly, Joseph pulled on a pair of thick socks and a flannel shirt. He rubbed his hands together and blew warm air across his knuckles. Then he pulled open the top drawer and inspected its contents. The soapstone seal, carved so many years ago as he sat alongside his father, the crumpled letter from Portland, and an assortment of bills and coins were all there as he expected.

He gathered the money from its envelope and spread it on the bed. Three twenties, two tens, three fives, six ones, and $3.53 in change. Joseph did the math in his head: $104.53 in all. It was not enough to pay both Mr. Nicholai and Mr. Townsend, but it was all he had. At least he'd have time now to check his snares. He might have a beaver pelt or two to sell. But the snares were probably buried deep beneath hard-packed drifts from the storm. Besides, both men wanted their payments today. A wave of discouragement overtook him.

Joseph pulled on a pair of jeans and shoved the money from the drawer into his pocket. He glanced at the lighted face of the alarm clock by the bed. It was too late now for a cup of tea or a piece of pilot bread. A blast of cold air came in with the slamming of the front door. All the others had apparently just left; only Joseph's mother sat at the kitchen table. She shook her head as he struggled with his parka, gloves, and hat. The sealskin parka was a concession to the frigid temperatures, but with it Joseph laced up his sneakers. They weren't much protection from the cold, but no one wore boots to school, no matter how cold it got.

Joseph had taken only a few steps before his feet began to tingle. The cold burned in his lungs, but the air was uncommonly still, so at least he didn't need to struggle against it for breath. In the gray edges of the morning, he saw thick white hoarfrost clinging to the frozen grasses and stubby willows that protruded here and there through the drifted snow. The day would be beautiful, though cold. And he would rather spend it in the frigid elements than in the confines of a building where he would encounter Elena and Mr. Townsend. Then there was Mr. Nicholai to face after school.

As he walked into the cold, Joseph weighed the options for his $104.53. Who should get the full amount owed? As if he actually owed either one, Joseph thought. Anger began to steam inside him, and Joseph struggled to think through it. Elena's father, at least, had merely made a mistake, jumped to a conclusion—with some help from Henry, of course. Maybe today he could find the words to reason with the storekeeper, or some other day, after the situation had cooled. But he would have to pay the full amount now, if the man was ever going to listen to reason. Mr. Townsend, on the other hand, was an outsider. In the end, neither his respect nor his disappointment meant much to Joseph. Yes, it was the white man who would have to get by with a partial payment.

Joseph looked up from his musings, relieved to have made his decision. The school building loomed before him, its edges and angles sharp and crisp looking in the cold, clear air. Simon was the one he met first, right inside the doorway, where the warm air embraced him.

"What's happening?" Simon asked.

"Aw, too much," Joseph answered, peeling off his winter gear. He wished he could feel the weight of his burdens removed like the weight of the heavy parka lifted from his shoulders. "There's a lot I haven't told you, Simon," he said quietly to his friend. The warning bell sounded in their ears. "Later today, let's talk." Joseph surprised himself with the suggestion, then managed a weak smile.

Simon wrinkled his nose and pushed up his glasses. "Right," he replied. "Later." He gave his friend a pat on the back, and they went off to their classroom.

In math, it was another day of struggling with letters and numbers. Next came science. Joseph saw when he entered the room that Mrs. Kingston had laid out lab stations for them. Elena was already there, but she turned her head and looked away when Joseph tried to catch her eye.

Mrs. Kingston told the students to each choose a lab partner, and Joseph considered a moment. Maybe if he went to Elena first and tried to tell his side of the story, she would listen. But when Elena saw him approach, she grabbed the hand of Elsie Charles and turned toward the nearest lab station.

So Joseph was stuck with Lott Alexie, another of the clan his family avoided. Lott didn't glare like Henry; in fact, he seemed oblivious to any conflict, turning all of his attention to making messes and annoying the girls working at the station beside them. He dripped water from an eyedropper down the back of Martha Henry's shirt and, when Mrs. Kingston was helping Elsie and Elena with the directions, he cranked the knob on their Bunsen burner to high, causing the girls to shriek at the searing flame. Mrs. Kingston turned and glared at the boys, but Elsie collected herself and adjusted the burner before any damage was done. Joseph, unamused, growled at his partner to stop fooling around but only got a test tube of water down his back in return. Anger flared up inside, but Joseph held it back. A year ago, he would have had fun with the same kind of antics. He glanced over at Elena and her partner, but their backs were turned and their heads bent intently over their experiment.

When the time finally came to clean up, Joseph hurriedly washed and wiped their work area and then looked over his shoulder at Elena. Elsie was back at her desk, charting the results of their work, and Elena was cleaning the counter alone. He set down his rag and hurried over to her.

"Elena," he said. He stood close. "I wanted to talk to you."

She scrubbed on, ignoring him.

"Elena, please." He tried not to plead, but he really wanted her to look at him. "It's important."

She stopped scrubbing and turned, looking him directly in the eye. He felt hot under her gaze but tried to hold it. "I have nothing to say to you." Her dark eyes danced, and anger seethed in her voice, barely more than a whisper.

"You don't have to say anything," he answered with an earnest whisper and stepped even closer. "I just want to explain."

Elena took a step back, still glaring. "You've done plenty of explaining to me," she hissed. "First it was about Mr. Townsend, then this job you needed so much. Don't you see what a fool you've made of me? I went out of my way to help you, to be your friend." Her eyes narrowed and she stepped back. "You took advantage of me and of my father. I want nothing more to do with you."

His eyes dropped. How could he make her understand? "Elena, please listen." He started again, but he heard her rag hit the counter and looked up to see her walking away. Before he could think, he heard his own

145

fist slam against the counter. She never looked back, and he turned away, his fist aching with the pain.

His soul felt drained empty as he sat like a rock while Mrs. Kingston wrapped up the lab results. How could you make someone listen to you? He thought of the pained look his mother would get whenever he turned away or stomped off, not wanting to hear her instructions or admonitions. Now he knew the inside aching that went with the look, a combination of pain and exasperation.

He tried to shift his emotions within, wanting to be angry with Elena for not hearing his side, but he kept returning to his hurt like a bird to its nest. He understood why she felt wounded. He tried telling himself that it didn't matter what she thought. He tried remembering Elena as he had known her before, with her shrill, whining voice and her pesky way of hanging around when he wanted to avoid her.

But he kept coming back to those nights on the steps, where she had sat close beside him, nodding in agreement over his concerns, and the days at the store when she would seek him out with a smile and a bit of conversation, and his talks with himself did nothing to ease the pain.

Not even a lively discussion in English class over misspent good intentions in *Romeo and Juliet* could rouse his interest. Joseph just wanted the day to be over. The money bulged in his pocket, but he realized that he didn't have the energy today to deal with explanations about the underpayment to Mr. Townsend.

When the bell rang, he started to his feet and headed

for the door, hoping the oversight of the expected payment would go unnoticed. But Mr. Townsend was too observant.

"Joseph," he called out, in a loud voice that Joseph couldn't ignore.

Slowly Joseph turned back toward the teacher's desk. He told himself to hold his head high, but it felt too heavy to lift.

"Joseph, it's the first Monday of the month. You have a payment for me, I believe." The teacher's voice was firm.

"Yeah, I do." Joseph fumbled in his pocket and thrust a twenty and a ten on Mr. Townsend's desk. With a deeper reach, he pulled out the assorted change, which jangled as it hit the hard surface.

Mr. Townsend frowned at the assorted coins. "You've had to dig deep this time," he said. "This doesn't look like fifty dollars."

"It isn't," Joseph mumbled.

"You've run up against a problem, then?" the teacher queried. There was no reply. "Joseph, if there's a problem, you need to tell me about it."

Joseph looked up, a scowl on his face. "Tell you about it? Like you're my friend or something?" He felt the familiar wrath rise in his throat as he took in the white hair, the blue eyes, the pale face.

"Yes, I think we should talk." Mr. Townsend's voice was calm and steady.

"Well, I don't." Anger whirled inside Joseph with an energy of its own, and his voice rose. "You're not my friend, you don't belong here, and I don't know why I ever agreed to this stupid deal in the first place. If the Fish and Game want to throw me in jail, let them come and get me." He controlled his voice just under the level of a shout, but inside he was raging.

Before the teacher could reply, Joseph turned and, at a half run, left the classroom. Mr. Townsend took a step after him, then stopped. Joseph continued on, his heart and his feet pounding. His pocket felt lighter already. Soon it would be empty, once he went by the store. Only his anger would be left unspent.

FOURTEEN

HIS DARK EYES FLASHING like the angry wind, Joseph pushed through the door of Nicholai's store. He scanned the area, and his eyes rested a moment on Henry Alexie, who was sweeping near the stairs. As if he sensed his cousin's glare, Henry looked up, and a twisted half smile crossed his face. Joseph felt hatred surge inside, and he mustered the strength to suppress it, to keep from striking out against this one who was, after all, one of his own people. He concentrated on regaining his focus. Mr. Nicholai—he had to pay him and be done—done with his job, with his obligations, with everything.

There he was, behind the glass window of his office, seated at his desk and bent over a calculator, punching in numbers. Joseph strode to the office door, forcing his gaze to rest on the store owner. Mr. Nicholai looked up.

"Joseph—" he began.

Joseph made no reply but thrust his hand in his pocket and pulled out the wad of bills.

"Here," he said, throwing the cash in front of the storekeeper, across the desktop. "It's all there."

Without waiting for a reply, Joseph turned and went out of the office and out of the store.

The air was still bitter, and the sun hung limply above the horizon. Joseph broke into a run. His sneakers pounded a rhythm into the boardwalk, and he felt himself begin to sweat even in the frigid air.

It seemed only moments before he reached his house. Joseph pushed open the doors, first of the porch, and then of the house. He flung his books across the weathered floor and glared at his mother, who sat cross-legged on the living-room bed.

He saw her flinch and turn away at the thud of his books on the floor. Then, without saying a word, she turned her attention back to the parka she was stitching. He watched as she pushed and tugged at the razor-edged skin-sewing needle.

Joseph looked about the shadowed room for another opportunity to vent the anger that still swelled within him, but no one else was home from school yet. The electric clock hummed quietly above the table where his mother sat. It was only a few minutes past noon. The others at school would be gathered in the gym, eating their lunches, maybe shooting a few baskets. Sam and the girls would not return home until after the sun had dipped below the horizon.

Joseph pushed his fingers through the tangle of his hair. He knew his mother must be wondering why he was home from school so early, but he also knew the cowered look he could raise with his anger. He needed to offer no explanation. Still, he had no desire to stay here, under her watchful eye. He pulled up the hood of his parka and went back through the outside door, letting it slam behind him. Then he stood for a moment in the receding sunlight and felt himself still seething with anger.

Part of him willed the anger to leave, but a stronger force clung to it, like the great snowdrifts that hold their form and resist the gentle urgings of a warm April sun. His anger, his hatred—they were too strong and too familiar to let go.

The school, the teacher, the Fish and Game—they were strangers here, just as his father had been. If he were a shaman like those in his grandfather's stories, he would change all the white-skinned men to white-headed eagles that would soar high above the village, and then he would slice their wings from their bodies so they would plummet to the ground. And the people of the village would tiptoe around them, pointing in horror, fearful of partaking of the tainted meat, leaving their twisted forms for the scavenging foxes.

But there was no longer any shaman's magic, only the schooling of the white man. Dull routines, endless rules, outside obligations piled one upon the other—burdens of progress that weighed upon Joseph's mind like his unpaid debt as he stood looking out across the frozen river, breathing heavy in the frosty air.

Joseph's troubles swirled within him like a backwater eddy—the money, his former job, his spoiled friendship with Elena, the intrusive school teacher. Anger at all of them frothed to the surface, and he broke into a dead run to escape it before it covered him completely.

As he ran, he thought of turning abruptly toward

his grandfather's house, of sitting in its warmth while Grandfather patiently listened to his woes. But his anger raged, too strong for such a settled end, and he continued off across the hard-packed snow, not caring if he followed any path, just wanting to get away.

Joseph was panting hard when he finally came to a stop at a ridge of higher ground far beyond the village. Heavy clouds hung above the land now, the frigid air filling fast with the promise of snow. Candy pink streaked the gray horizon, meeting with spindly willows that lined the far ridge.

Drenched in sweat, Joseph felt the chill of the afternoon air seep around his face and through his flimsy sneakers. Bending at the waist, his hands on his knees, Joseph caught his breath. His mind told him to stop this foolish running, but his body was still wound tight with anger.

Joseph began to run again. He was going nowhere, only away, away from the ruined world, the havoc wreaked in his life by white men, havoc that began with his own conception and birth.

He looked to the side as he ran and saw the distant winter sun hovering just at the horizon. The ridge had become gray-black like the sky. Joseph's run slowed to a steady beat, and his lungs burned heavy with breathing, the only sound in the hushed, flat landscape. As he pushed on, his chest heaving and burning with the exertion, he wondered how far he had run without a trail across the packed snow. A moment of panic set in, and he looked frantically from side to side for landmarks.

But his feet still carried him forward with a compulsion all their own.

His worry was uncalled for. Just to his right loomed the familiar expanse of Igayik Lake, calling out to him in another wave of anger with the memory of his fall hunt, ruined by the teacher.

Joseph's pounding feet reached the edge of the lake and hit the thinly crusted ice. It's just the overflow, he told himself. Too late, he heard a booming crack, too loud to be only the crust of overflow breaking. Suddenly he felt the weight of his body pulling him down through the icy water. He seemed suspended for a moment in time, and then he felt the mucky bottom sucking at the soles of his sneakers. Waves of fear flowed over him like the lake water, and he pushed frantically to the surface toward the circle of light where he had broken through.

He had been under water for only a few seconds. Now he gasped at the frigid air. All around him, the ice cracked unforgivingly as he tried to slide up onto it, willing his weight to distribute itself evenly. But with his every attempt to get the ice to hold him, Joseph found that the lake's wound grew wider still. He would have to reach the bank, to get on solid ground, if he was to have any hope of survival.

Joseph began reaching purposefully now in the direction of the shore. The ice continued to crack as he spread himself across it, but he pushed his panic aside. Finally he was able to grab a small willow on the lake's edge. Joseph wrenched his body upward, but the sapling snapped under his weight. As the waterlogged heaviness of his clothing pulled him down again, the force of his spent anger resurrected itself as a force of terror. He looked about and grabbed once more with both hands, this time at a sturdier branch of many winters.

All the muscles in his arms tensed against the pull of the heavy wetness. His grasp grew weak, and his right hand slipped. Frantically, he reached again, all the while feeling the weakness of his left hand, which certainly could not hold him for long. His right hand brushed the branch, but his grasping fingers missed it. A wave of discouragement overcame him; the weight of his wet parka, his sneakers, his whole body—it was too much. Yet he knew he could not give in so easily, not without his greatest effort. He reached again, his eyes fixed on the branch. This time his right hand grasped it firmly. He felt a surge of strength in both arms, and, slowly, he hoisted himself onto the bank.

Joseph sat on the crusted snow, the drips on his parka already suspended in ice. He panted and gasped at the welcome air, never minding its cold. He had succeeded, outwitting the cruel grasp of nature, so ready to take advantage of his carelessness. But he was not a careless person, Joseph told himself. No Real Person could afford to be careless against the elements.

With this thought, the pounding of his heart and his anger at Mr. Townsend throbbed inside. Wasn't the teacher the cause of all of this—the brush with death, the drenched hand-sewn furs, the panic and struggle? There was so much Joseph wanted to say, to release against the intruder—so much he could never say.

Joseph turned his face into the wind and yelled his frustration, commanding the wind to take his anger and his distress to the ocean so that he could return, purged and cleansed, to his home and start again. But his scream echoed emptily against the ridge, and Joseph was conscious only of the chilled air that engulfed him.

Joseph rose and turned in the direction of the village, feeling inside as heavy as his wet parka. He began to walk, forcing each foot forward, willing himself not to lag or stumble. But the cold bit through with each step. The lake was still visible over his shoulder when his feet began to grow numb. He kept moving forward until he could no longer see the lake when he looked back, and so he only looked forward into the graying night. Before long his mind began to grow numb and fuzzy, and his sense of purpose faltered.

He wandered, putting one foot in front of the other, for what seemed like hours. Each step crunched a rhythm in the snow, over and over until the noise became his only awareness. He mind grew strangely empty, and his feet lost all sensation. He felt suspended in time, utterly alone and without purpose.

Then, gripped by a moment of reality, he found himself back where he had started, at the gaping hole in the lake ice, an angry circle that mirrored the angry circle he had trod in the snow. His heart sank with the weight of despair as he looked over the darkened lake.

The survival teachings of his grandfather and of the schoolbooks called to him faintly. He should look at the emerging stars to get his bearings. He should walk faster, to keep his blood warm. He should stay focused on his family and friends, vibrant and alive, waiting for him in the village. But he was so tired and cold.

He sat at the edge of the lake. He felt as if a peace, a calm, lay just beyond his reach. He wanted to lie back into the snow, to close his eyes, to rest just for a while. Just for a while—to collect his thoughts.

Something deep within him cried out against the impulse. He must not rest; he must not give up. *Never give up.* They were his father's words, recalled from deep in the past.

He must have been about Sam's age, six or seven, at the time. He had been struggling with his pocketknife, clumsily chiseling into a hunk of black soapstone. His knife left crude, sharp edges in the stone, not smooth curves like his father could make. Joseph's eyes had burned hot with tears, and he had thrown down the knife and the half-finished seal carving.

His father had leaned over and picked up both tool and carving. He handed them to Joseph and, in a quiet voice, reminded him, "Never give up." Now, lost in the cold of a winter night, Joseph tried to push these words out of remembrance. They were false words from a man who had given up on everything—the village, his wife, and his children.

Joseph looked up to see eerie green fingers of light pushing toward earth from the darkening sky. He watched as they danced with glee, playfully touching first here and then there. He remembered another time when he had watched northern lights, sitting beside Elena on her steps in the cool, late autumn air after work one night. He had wondered then if the lights would ever again seem so brilliant.

With the last threads of consciousness, Joseph knew that now these lights were reaching for him, trying to snatch him away to the beyond. Whistle, whistle as Grandfather taught, scare them away, he told himself. But try as he might, he could not bring a whistle from his stiff lips.

Then, from the recesses of his numbed mind, he heard the teacher's voice: "Rage, rage against the dying of the light." But his rage was all spent.

A calm settled in, and Joseph lay back. The last thought he remembered was the hope that the calm would stay forever, and he would rage no more.

Joseph sensed his nakedness and the warmth surrounding him, and wondered if this was how one passed into the world beyond. He blinked open his eyes, fearful yet curious, to gaze upon the unknown. But his eyes met the deep blue of the schoolteacher's eyes, and Joseph was confused.

"He's coming out of it," exclaimed Mr. Townsend, turning toward the slight figure seated beside the bed. Joseph moved his head a bit and saw that the figure was his grandfather, looking bent and frail, smiling and nodding his approval.

"You had passed out from hypothermia when we found you," Mr. Townsend explained. "Your temperature had dropped so low that we thought we had lost you for awhile."

"You—you found me? Lost me?" Joseph's head

pounded as he tried to lift it up. The teacher gently pushed him back.

"Just rest now," he said.

Joseph closed his eyes and struggled to remember. The anger, his pounding feet, the wet and cold, the circle—there had been a flurry of events. But now he felt only calm, and he savored it as he drifted back to sleep.

FIFTEEN

WHEN JOSEPH AWOKE AGAIN, the gray light of morning was streaking through the curtains of the window beside the bed. He glanced about, struggling to recall where he was and why. It had been fully dark when he had wakened before. Now his grandfather dozed in a hard wooden chair. Joseph felt a twinge of guilt with the realization that he occupied the only bed in his grandfather's tiny home.

Joseph propped himself on his elbows and looked more closely at the room. There was the table, the CB, the tiny oil stove, a counter and basin, and a shelf holding canned goods. It was the same as always. Somehow, he had expected it would be different.

His grandfather's chin lifted and his eyes opened, the lids still heavy with sleep.

"So you have returned to us, Joseph," he said. The Yup'ik words made a gentle melody in the morning quiet.

Joseph lay his head back on the pillow. Every muscle felt tired. "I'm so ashamed, Grandfather," he said. "I forgot all that you taught me and wandered in a circle. And taking off running like that— It was so foolish." The shortcomings were whispered, but his grandfather heard and nodded.

"Yes, foolish," he concurred. "What made you run?"

Joseph probed about within for the strong feelings that had led him to such rash action. Had it been only the day before? The raging fury had shrunk to a tiny ember, but Joseph remembered how it had burned.

"I was angry, so angry," he replied.

Grandfather nodded again. "Your teacher—what is his name? He thought so."

The white-haired man had been there, Joseph recalled, smiling and speaking in soothing tones. Had it been in this very room? "Mr. Townsend," he informed his grandfather. "He was here, wasn't he?"

"Iii," Grandfather affirmed.

"But why?" Joseph asked.

Grandfather coughed, a loose rattle shaking his chest. "He had gone to your mother's house looking for you after school. He said you had run off and not returned to the building, so he grew concerned. Your mother said she had seen you only briefly and told him that you might be here with me."

The old man paused a moment. He stretched his arms and legs out before him, flexing each limb slowly. Then he continued. "Your teacher headed toward my house, noticing even in the twilight some sneaker prints veering out into the open snow." A smile lit his face, and he nodded toward the oil stove. Joseph's sneakers sat on the floor beside the stove, laces hanging limply. "Those sneakers—what Eskimo wears sneakers on the frozen tundra?" Grandfather laughed and set a hand on Joseph's arm.

He lifted himself slowly from the chair and ambled to

the stove. Joseph's dark eyes followed him. "And what happened then, Grandfather—after he came to your house?"

Grandfather took a tea bag and mug from the shelf above the stove. He poured steaming water from the kettle into the mug and then maneuvered back to the chair, his feet making light shuffling sounds as he went. He dipped the tea bag up and down slowly, watching it all the while. Joseph waited silently until his grandfather retrieved the thread of his story.

"When the teacher discovered that you were not here, he suggested that we go back and follow the footprints. He left to get his snow machine, and when he returned, we went out together to find you."

"You and Mr. Townsend went out together on the snow machine?" Joseph tried to imagine the unlikely pair on the machine as it bounced a path over the open tundra.

"We followed your footsteps to near the ridge and then over to Igayik Lake. We found you there, huddled over against the snowbank." Grandfather paused and removed the tea bag, waiting for the excess tea to drip out before setting the bag on the window ledge. He looked out across the room, away from Joseph, and blinked several times.

"We thought you might be dead," he said, his voice barely more than a whisper. "But the teacher took your pulse and felt your breath. He wrapped you in a wool blanket and set you on the machine between us." Grandfather turned and looked at Joseph, long and penetrating. Then a smile broke over his face. "Good thing he has a long-track Ski-doo."

Joseph returned the smile, but inside his heart sank. He had caused so much hurt to his grandfather, who had taken care to watch over and teach him since he was young.

Grandfather continued. "When we returned here, your mother was waiting. She was very worried about you, Joseph."

Joseph nodded, feeling lower still.

"She stripped you down, and we warmed you slowly, here in my bed. Then we waited—two, maybe three hours. Your color returned and your breathing grew deeper. Even your feet suffered only a little frostbite. You must have run very hard."

Joseph nodded his reply again. He wiggled his toes beneath the blankets, thankful that they still moved.

"So," Grandfather continued, "your mother went home to be with your sisters and brother. Sam had been crying, asking for you."

Joseph turned away, blinking fiercely. Silence overtook the room, and Grandfather sipped at his tea.

"Your teacher—he stayed, though. He stayed until you woke up, in the very early morning," Grandfather commented.

My teacher, Joseph thought. The kass'aq teacher, my enemy—he stayed. He looked for me, he found me, he stayed with me—here in Grandfather's plywood house, when he could have been sleeping soundly in his warm teacher's house. Why would he do this?

As if Grandfather could read his thoughts, he added, "I think you owe this man your life, Joseph." It was a matter-of-fact statement, simple and direct. Having said it, Grandfather swallowed the last of his tea and set the mug at his feet.

Joseph said nothing, but his thoughts were spinning faster now. This was a huge debt, his life owed to this kass'aq man, much bigger than the debt that he owed to the Fish and Game. The debt of money he resented but had paid reluctantly because he was caught and trapped. This new debt, he wasn't sure about. He felt something of a scowl cross his face as he turned the thoughts around in his mind.

His grandfather was watching him. "So, you are not too fond of this Mr. Townsend?" he asked.

"No—well, yes—I mean, I don't really know, Ap'a," Joseph admitted. "I don't really know him."

"Iii," Grandfather said. "Perhaps now you will know him better. Sometimes we chase off those we don't know before we really should."

Joseph closed his eyes. The image from his dream, chasing and being chased, flashed through his mind. Opening his eyes, Joseph saw that his grandfather had settled back in silence. The teakettle steamed softly on the oil stove, and the clock ticked loudly on the wall.

A gnawing in his stomach turned Joseph's thoughts away from his circle of problems. "Ap'a," he asked. "Could I have a cup of tea with sugar? And some dry fish, if you have it?"

The old man nodded and went to the cupboard, retrieving another mug and some oily strips of dry fish. He dumped two teaspoons of sugar into the mug along with the tea bag, added water from the kettle, and brought the strips and mug to Joseph's bedside. He set them on the tiny nightstand and helped Joseph to prop the pillow behind him so that he could lean against the chilly wall.

The meal tasted as good as any Joseph had ever eaten. He sipped at the hot, sweet tea, which soothed his dry throat. Between sips, he filled his mouth with the familiar smoky flavor of the dried salmon that he stripped from the skin with his teeth and chewed with vigor.

He had nearly finished when footsteps sounded on the porch. There was a light stomping off of snow, and then the door creaked open slowly.

"Joseph?" It was Elena's soft voice.

His grandfather spoke as he stood up from the chair. "Come," he said. "Sit." He motioned to the wooden chair by the bed.

Elena removed her coat and gloves. They were already dripping in the warm household air. Her eyes widened with concern as they settled on Joseph, stretched out in his grandfather's bed.

Joseph quickly swallowed and pulled the covers up to his chest, rubbing his fingers on the underside of the sheet to remove the remaining fish oil.

Elena came to his side. She looked intently at Joseph and reached as if to take his hand. Then she drew back.

Grandfather cleared his throat. "I'll go now to tell your mother that you're fully awake and have eaten. She will be relieved to hear it." He smiled slightly and turned toward the porch. For a moment, there was only the sound of him putting on his boots, his coat, his gloves, his hat. Then the outside door slammed lightly shut, and Elena and Joseph were alone.

"Joseph, I was so worried about you when it came over the CB that you'd been out alone, half the night, in that freezing cold," Elena said.

Joseph smiled weakly, meeting her gaze. "You were angry with me, though," he reminded her.

Elena looked down, and her face flushed with a tinge of pink. "I was," she admitted. "And I thought I had good reason to be. But it occurred to me later, when I heard you were missing, that I never gave you a chance to explain." She paused, swallowed hard, and looked up at Joseph.

"And then I was so afraid that you would not be found, and I wouldn't ever be able to give you a chance." A weak smile crossed her face.

Joseph reached out and took her hand in his. She looked up. "I'm not sure I deserve a chance, Elena," Joseph said softly. "I let you down before when you believed me. How could you trust me?"

Joseph paused. It was a bigger problem than he had realized. How do you earn someone's trust when you've already had it once and lost it? He struggled for the right words.

"Even so, I want to tell you the truth and hope you'll believe it's so. I didn't steal that money from the register. Henry did see me open the drawer, but only to put in a twenty-dollar bill I found on the floor." He paused a moment. How much should he tell? Gently, Elena squeezed his hand. He took a deep breath and continued.

"I admit, I did think about keeping that twenty dollars, but only for a minute. Obviously it belonged in the

165

register. I couldn't steal from your dad after he gave me a job and all."

Elena looked puzzled. "But what about the hundred and fifty dollars?" she asked.

Joseph cleared his throat. "I really don't know for sure," he said, "but I think it was Henry. The way he looked at me—I don't know—it made me suspicious. He never has liked me."

"And you've never liked him," Elena reminded him. "You could be pinning this all on him."

Joseph sighed. "Yes, I guess that's true," he admitted. "But since the feeling is mutual, he has a motive, too. I think that now he's a hundred and fifty dollars richer, plus he's got the satisfaction of knowing he blamed the theft on me."

Elena looked away and was silent a moment. Joseph studied her face, wondering whether she believed him. Suddenly, he noticed.

"Elena, your face!" He blurted it out without thinking.

Elena's hands flew to her face, palms on her cheeks. "What?" she cried, turning toward Joseph.

Joseph realized what he had done, but it was too late to back out now. It was his turn to blush. "It's just that—well—it's your makeup." Elena's brows furrowed, trying to figure. "I mean, you're not wearing any, and it's a school day."

Elena covered her mouth with her hands.

Joseph grinned. "No, don't be alarmed," he said. "I like you much better without it."

"You do?" Elena let her hands fall, and a smile edged across her face.

"Yes," Joseph affirmed. He studied her a moment. "Your eyes, your mouth, your skin—I can see the real you. And—you're really very pretty."

"Joseph!" she said, and her gaze dropped to the floor as color rose to her cheeks.

Joseph could tell she was pleased. Still, there was more to be said.

"Elena," he said in a serious tone. "I want to tell you something else."

She looked up, her eyes questioning.

"The money I told you I needed," Joseph said. She nodded. "Well, it wasn't for a sewing machine for my mom like I told you. I mean, if I had enough, I would have gotten her one, but first I had to pay the troopers."

"The troopers?" Elena asked. Her eyes were big again.

"Remember when the Fish and Game troopers found their airplane tires slashed?" Joseph paused. He was in too deep not to confess all. "Well, I'm the one who did it."

"Joseph—" Her voice was stern, like a scolding mother.

"I'm not proud of it now. I was angry—but I guess that's no excuse."

"Did you get caught, then?" Elena asked. He imagined she was puzzled that she hadn't heard about it.

"Sort of. Mr. Townsend was on the tundra at the time, and he saw me. He told the troopers he knew who did it, but he wouldn't tell them my name."

"Why not?" she asked.

"I really don't know," Joseph admitted. Funny, he hadn't given that aspect of the situation much thought.

"Anyway, he worked out this deal, where I would pay him fifty dollars on the first and third Mondays of each month, and he would pass it on to the troopers. That way I wouldn't get in big trouble, but the debt would be paid."

"Wow," Elena said. "I didn't know Mr. Townsend was such a nice guy."

"I never really thought of him that way," Joseph admitted. "I got so mad at him sometimes. Like when I was duck hunting—"

"Now do I get to hear what *really* happened?" Elena interrupted.

"Yes," said Joseph firmly. He was starting to feel light and airy, as if a huge burden was lifting from his body. "He did interrupt my hunt, but he didn't waste any birds, unless you want to count the one that I shot at when it was too far away. That's the one I couldn't find, even though I looked all morning. That was sort of his fault, because he disturbed me and all."

"It sounds like it was sort of—or maybe mostly—your fault, Joseph," Elena chided.

Joseph thought a moment and nodded slightly. "Well, I suppose so. I don't know why I told you different from what really happened. I guess I wanted to get back at him."

Elena's eyes narrowed and she moved in closer to Joseph. "Joseph Benchley," she said, "I shouldn't believe a single word you say, after all of this." Then her face lit in a smile. "But, for some reason, I do. Maybe it's because you're telling me things that are difficult to admit. I do believe you."

Joseph smiled. His relief felt complete, or almost so. "Elena?" he said.

"What?"

"Thanks."

"I just want to be able to trust you from now on," Elena added.

"You can," Joseph said, his voice firm and confident.

Elena glanced at the clock. "Eleven thirty—I'd better get back to school and tell everyone how you're doing," she said. "Mr. Townsend said I could come over during class to find out." She reached for her coat and gloves. Once she had them on, she smiled once more at Joseph.

"Get better soon, OK?"

Joseph nodded and watched as she went out the door. If she could forgive him, perhaps all was not lost.

SIXTEEN

"LOST SOULS," Simon's father was saying. Joseph had heard the preaching before, but the words had a new impact now that he had been lost on the winter tundra. He shifted his weight on the hard pew where he sat next to Simon. The air had settled into layers around them—frosty at the wooden floor, warm with body heat above. The freestanding oil furnace in the back of the church labored and moaned with the stress of trying to keep up with its task.

Joseph heard the door creak open in the back. A late-comer let in a blast of cold air, temporarily displacing some of the warmth. Simon's father droned on, "Lost souls, caught in the web of sin, a savior . . ." Joseph looked over at Simon, who stifled a yawn, and then returned his focus to the preacher. He tried to force his ears to hear the words, but noises seemed to tumble indiscriminately from all directions—the wail of a baby, children scuffling in another pew, the creaking old furnace, the wind whistling along the windowsills.

The morning light bathed the sparse interior walls with a harsh glow, casting a tinge of winter gray on all the living souls within. Joseph closed his eyes. This group of people at the church was the first he'd been with since his rescue. For days, he had lain in bed, resting, eating, regaining his strength, first at his grandfather's house and then at his own.

And he had been thinking all the while. Sometimes the thoughts seemed to swallow him, but he forced himself to deal with them: what had happened, what might have happened, the debts he owed, the anger inside, the kass'aq intrusion, his father. There were no easy solutions, but in those days of total quiet he waded through all his problems. He simply turned over and fell asleep whenever he became overwhelmed.

He couldn't honestly say that he'd arrived at any answers, but he managed to look squarely at his anger. Had it been justified? Yes, he decided—to a certain extent. But to let it consume him—this was the error he must avoid. How he would accomplish this was still a puzzle to him.

At any rate, tomorrow he would go back to school. He would face his classmates and their questions. He would face Mr. Townsend. He still wasn't sure exactly what he would say.

A creak and a blast of cold air signaled the arrival of yet another latecomer, though the service was more than half over. Joseph turned to look, and a flash of white hair caught his eye as the worshiper pulled off his hat and took a seat in the third pew from the back. He had never seen Mr. Townsend in church before; his pale face stuck out among all the native faces. Joseph's heart beat faster with the realization that he might have to speak with the teacher now, before he really knew what to say.

The congregation rose to its feet, and Joseph, though he had missed the instruction to do so, rose with them. He took a moment to look around at the faces in the pews behind him. There was Peter Angaiak, standing with hunched shoulders next to his grown daughter, Florence. Behind them stood Alexie John, his round face fixed firmly toward the front of the church. Over to the left was Nastasia Paniak, looking fatter than ever beneath a fur-lined *qaspeq*. And beside her stood thin-faced Gertrude Nicholai, her stern husband Robert, and their girls, including Elena, who caught Joseph's eye and smiled.

The piano sounded a few notes, and Joseph turned back toward the front. The singing began, a Yup'ik version of "Just As I Am," translated decades before by missionaries who had labored to capture the lilting language into written form so that the gospel and hymns could be shared. Joseph had sung the English words before, but the Yup'ik had a more soulful sound that spoke closer to his heart. He joined in the chorus, softly at first, then with more resonance.

He wondered what Mr. Townsend was doing as they sang in what for him was a foreign tongue. Joseph turned again for a discreet look. The teacher was singing, too, but the words formed by his lips didn't match the others, as if he were part of a poorly synchronized video. Joseph turned his head quickly back toward the front. Evidently Mr. Townsend was singing the English words with an indiscernible voice that agreed in melody and meaning with the resonating Yup'ik song.

The hymn came to an end, and the congregation remained standing. "Please join me," Simon's father said, in English now, "in saying the Lord's Prayer."

Joseph joined in, his voice softly repeating the familiar words. "Our Father . . . hallowed be thy name . . . thy will be done . . . give us this day . . . forgive us our trespasses, as we forgive those who trespass against us."

These words stuck in Joseph's throat. The congregation went on, but he forced himself to repeat this line. "Forgive us our trespasses, as we forgive those who trespass against us." Elena had forgiven him. That was something. But more was needed. Joseph knew this in his heart, but the details eluded him. The box of trespasses—he had finally begun to open it. But forgiving those who had trespassed against him—this concept began to turn slowly in his mind as the congregation said "Amen" and took their seats.

The service wound to a close with the usual formalities: another song, a prayer of benediction, the dismissal. Joseph was thinking all the while.

"Let's get out of here." Joseph mouthed the words to Simon, and his friend nodded. The room seemed stifling now, and the fresh air beckoned outdoors. The boys slid quickly to the aisle and made their way to the door.

Old Nastasia hobbled in front of them, and they slowed their rush. The old woman reached out a hand to grab the arm of Hannah Sam, another round, gray-haired woman, and the aisle was momentarily blocked. The boys stopped completely.

Suddenly, Joseph heard a firm voice. "Joseph." It was Mr. Townsend. Joseph turned, and all his energy pulled toward his heart, which thumped wildly. He looked down.

"I'm glad to see you're doing so much better. Your friends tell me you'll be in school tomorrow," the teacher said.

"Yes," Joseph answered softly. He raised his eyes to look at the teacher.

"So," Mr. Townsend continued, "I guess you'll have a lot of work to make up."

Joseph smiled weakly and nodded. Then it could just be like this, everything back to normal, except more polite and guarded.

Joseph turned to continue down the aisle. Now is the time, a voice inside said, now is the time, if you're going to do this thing.

He turned back. "Mr. Townsend?"

"Yes?" The teacher looked him full in the face.

"I need to say, or ask, something." The words came hard, but he pushed them out. This was harder than he had imagined when he was sitting in the pew. "First, I want to thank you for what you did the other night. If you hadn't come looking for me, well, I guess I'd probably be dead."

Mr. Townsend nodded and put his hand on Joseph's shoulder. "I'm glad I went looking, too. I didn't want to intrude, but something seemed very wrong."

"It was," Joseph agreed. "I mean, I was upset about not having the money and all. Someone accused me of stealing at the store, and I lost my job. I gave you all I could. I knew it wasn't enough, but there was nothing I could do to fix it."

Mr. Townsend let his hand fall to his side. "If you

would have told me this at the time, I'm sure we could have worked something out." His voice was gently chiding. A tiny ripple of irritation rose within Joseph, but he squelched it. Calm, he told himself. He took a deep breath and searched his mind for more words.

"I was so angry," Joseph explained. "It was like a dam had been building inside me for a long time, and right then it gave way."

Mr. Townsend nodded and kept his gaze on Joseph. The after-church voices formed a humming backdrop. Joseph was aware of Simon, not right at his side, but a respectful distance away now. Joseph wondered if his friend could hear his confessions. He took a deep breath and continued.

"I was angry with you, angry because you caught me, angry because you're a kass'aq. And once when I was hunting . . ."

Mr. Townsend raised an eyebrow quizzically. For Joseph, this was the hardest part of all.

"Once when I was hunting, you motored in just as I was about to shoot. You ruined my shot, or anyway my shot was ruined, and I couldn't find the bird that fell." The silence, even with the crowd nearby, seemed enormous.

"And then," Mr. Townsend prodded.

"And then I told Elena that story about you. She told lots of other people, but it wasn't her fault. She believed me." Joseph paused. This was so hard. "I know it did a lot of damage to your reputation, and I just want you to know that I'm sorry. I hope you will forgive me." The last part was almost a whisper, but he said it.

The teacher opened his mouth, as if to reply, but then

closed it without a sound. They stood for a moment, teacher and student, enveloped in their own layer of silence.

Then the white man reached out to clasp Joseph's hand in a kass'aq-style handshake. His manner was firm. "I do forgive you, Joseph," he said quietly.

Mr. Townsend reached for his hat. He nodded at Joseph and Simon and said, "See you tomorrow."

Relief swept in like the wake of a boat. Joseph turned to Simon, who was already heading toward the door of the fast-emptying church. The cold air wakened all of their senses as they met it outside, its powerful presence engulfing the village, so tiny against the vast winter scape.

"Did you hear what we were saying?" Joseph asked his friend.

Simon nodded. "I hope you don't mind. But I am your friend, you know."

"You're a good one, too," Joseph said. "You've been through a lot with me."

They walked in silence to where the church board-walk met the main path.

"Hey," said Simon. The familiar grin was back. "Come to my house and my mom will feed you duck soup."

Hunger gnawed at Joseph's belly, and he could almost taste the hearty broth. But there was something else calling to him with unexpected urgency.

"Thanks, but there's something I need to do," Joseph said. Now, he added to himself, before I lose my resolve. "And besides, there's a feast at my aunt's house—her son's birthday," he added.

"OK. More at home for me then," Simon said with a grin. He turned off to the right, leaving Joseph to walk home alone.

Joseph set off toward his house. Most of the ice from autumn's indecisive weather had worn off the board-walk now, and he was able to stride quickly along. He broke into a run. By the time he reached his front door, he was breathing heavy with exertion, but his head was clear and his body alive with purpose.

Joseph went in, first through the dark entryway and then into the house. Silence met him there; it seemed to prod him on. The rest of the family had evidently gone straight to his aunt's house after church. He could join them shortly. Right now, he was grateful for the peace that enveloped him in the cluttered room.

Joseph removed his hat and coat, leaving them in a pile by the door. He went to the bedroom and opened his top dresser drawer. It was empty of money, of course. He lifted the half-finished soapstone seal and cradled it a moment in his hand, stroking the rough edges and smooth planes. Then he set it gently back in the drawer and pulled out the crumpled envelope.

It took only a moment to rummage through his pack for a pen and a piece of lined paper. Then Joseph sat at the table. He pushed aside two mugs and a plastic bag of dry fish, and he drew in a deep breath. He began to write.

Dear Dad,

I got your letter a long time ago, but it has taken me awhile to try to answer. Much has happened to me in the past few weeks.

I guess you know from the girls that we've done all right since you left. Mom is fine, and so are the girls and Sam. Or maybe you don't even know about Sam. He was born a few months after you left. He looks a lot like me, with dark, wavy hair, and he's kind of tall compared with the other kids around here. I used to hate that, looking so kass'aq, but Sam doesn't seem to notice yet. Maybe he never will.

Anyway, I have one thing I really need to say in this letter. I have been angry with you ever since you left. To me, you have been an enemy, not a father. With my anger, I wanted to hurt you, but now I see that hurting you wouldn't fix anything.

I want to forgive you, Dad. I'm not certain I can, but I want to try. So that's why I had to write this letter.

Oh, and about this summer. If you really have the money to buy me a ticket, maybe I could come for a week or two, as long as it's in between fish runs. Mom and Grandfather count on me for fishing.

> Your son,
> Joseph

Joseph put his pen down. He reread the letter slowly. Yes, it was what he wanted to say. He folded the paper carefully in thirds and dug in the kitchen drawer for an envelope. Carefully, he inserted the letter. Then he copied the Portland address. He took a deep breath, sealed the envelope, and stuck it in his pack. He would take it to the post office tomorrow after school.

For now, hunger called. He had passed up the duck soup. He hoped his aunt had something equally good, topped off with creamy Eskimo ice cream, loaded with berries from the freezer for this special occasion.

He stopped at the basin and checked in the mirror. He reached for a comb to settle the stray hairs into gentle waves. He would always look part kass'aq, he told himself, never exactly full Yup'ik like everyone else. He wasn't sure of what all of the kass'aq part entailed. Maybe if he visited his dad, it would become clearer.

But no matter what, he realized as he took one last look at himself, his life was full of the richness of the Yup'ik ways. He vowed then and there, to himself in the mirror, always to cling to them, not out of defiance for his enemies, but out of love for his people—the Real People.

Joseph's stomach rumbled, calling him to the reality of the moment. He pulled on his hat and coat and ambled into the daylight. He stopped on the steps and surveyed his world. Sun had broken through a hole in the clouds, and the snow on the frozen river ice sparkled a thousand promises to the young man. He breathed in the freshness of the day. Then he set off to join the feast.

Deb Vanasse began her career as an English teacher in three tiny villages in Alaska that were just opening high schools. She became interested in the strong traditions the Yup'ik people tried to retain while being bombarded by outside change. Her inspiration to write about these experiences produced a short story, which eventually became *A Distant Enemy*, her first novel.

She lives with her husband and two teenage children in Fairbanks, Alaska.